THE HACKER

NORCROSS SECURITY #5

ANNA HACKETT

The Hacker

Published by Anna Hackett

Copyright 2021 by Anna Hackett

Cover by Lana Pecherczyk

Cover image by Paul Henry Serres

Edits by Tanya Saari

ISBN (ebook): 978-1-922414-38-0

ISBN (paperback): 978-1-922414-39-7

Heart of Eon - Romantic Book of the Year (Ruby) winner 2020

Cyborg - PRISM Award Winner 2019

Edge of Eon and Mission: Her Protection - Romantic Book of the Year (Ruby) finalists 2019

Unfathomed and Unmapped - Romantic Book of the Year (Ruby) finalists 2018

Unexplored – Romantic Book of the Year (Ruby) Novella Winner 2017

Return to Dark Earth – One of Library Journal's Best E-Original Books for 2015 and two-time SFR Galaxy Awards winner

At Star's End – One of Library Journal's Best E-Original Romances for 2014

The Phoenix Adventures – SFR Galaxy Award Winner for Most Fun New Series and "Why Isn't This a Movie?" Series

Beneath a Trojan Moon – SFR Galaxy Award Winner and RWAus Ella Award Winner

Hell Squad – SFR Galaxy Award for best Post-Apocalypse for Readers who don't like Post-Apocalypse

"Like Indiana Jones meets Star Wars. A treasure hunt with a steamy romance." – SFF Dragon, review of *Among Galactic Ruins*

"Action, danger, aliens, romance – yup, it's another great book from Anna Hackett!" – Book Gannet Reviews, review of *Hell Squad: Marcus*

Sign up for my VIP mailing list and get your *free box set* containing three action-packed romances.

Visit here to get started: www.annahackett.com

CHAPTER ONE

The drone buzzed overhead.

Looking at the screen on her controller, Maggie Lopez finessed the controls. The footage of the forest looked great. She grinned. She had several clients who'd potentially be interested in it, or she could upload it to her stock video site. She flew the drone higher, swiveling the camera.

She was standing in a clearing of the Muir Woods National Monument in the Golden Gate National Recreation Area, north of the Golden Gate Bridge. *There.* That was the money shot.

The view down to the coast and the beaches was beautiful.

She flew the drone back and whizzed over some people below—hikers, tourists, perhaps the three scientists she'd brought here in her helicopter. She was lucky to have the special permits to fly her drone here.

The three men were a grumpy lot and didn't say much, but they'd paid upfront so they could spend several hours looking at redwoods. It was no skin off her nose.

She brought a drone into a smooth landing on the grass in front of her. Time to pack up. She glanced at her chunky Hugo Boss watch. The scientists would be back soon.

She pulled the drone apart and packed it into the large case she'd left out. Once everything was in place, she closed the lid and lifted the box. She slid it into the cargo area at the back of the Bell 407 helicopter that was her baby. She'd risked everything to buy Hetty, short for Henrietta.

Then Maggie hesitated. *Shit.* Should she be lifting boxes?

She closed her eyes and slid her hand into the pocket of her jeans. She pulled out the small piece of plastic she'd been carrying around for the last week.

Her stomach did a tap dance and her mouth went dry.

She stared at the two lines.

Yep, still pregnant.

She rubbed her cheek. One month ago, she'd made a big mistake. Okay, it'd also been a thrilling, sexy, multi-orgasmic mistake, but a mistake all the same.

She'd slept with a hot, sexy man who she'd secretly been crushing on forever. A man who was smart, funny, loyal...but who also loved women. A great variety of women.

Ace Oliveira.

Even now, Maggie felt her blood heat. He worked for Norcross Security as their tech guru. A former NSA operative, the man could do things with computers that most people didn't even know were possible.

She was on retainer to Norcross as their pilot when they needed a helo ride. She blew out a breath. The boss man, Vander Norcross, had lured her out of the Navy. They'd met a few years back, when she'd flown a Seahawk from her aircraft carrier to rescue his Ghost Ops team from a mission that had gone fubar. They'd been under fire, and she'd done some fancy flying to get them all out of there alive.

Now, she had her own budding business in Dragonfly Aerial—and the debt to prove it. Plus, she got to keep her flying skills sharp when the Norcross badasses had a job.

It also looked like she was going to have a baby in less than nine months.

Dios. She leaned against the side of her helicopter. What the hell was she going to do? She hadn't told her parents yet. Hell, she hadn't told Ace yet. Her belly tried to turn itself inside out.

She hadn't seen him since that night. She bit her lip and slid both her hands into her pockets, tucking the plastic away at the same time.

Even now, she remembered every second in brilliant, spine-tingling detail.

They'd been at a fancy event—a big jewelry gala. Norcross' main bodyguard, Rome Nash, had been guarding the sponsor of the event: Princess Sofia of Caldova.

Maggie had dressed up for the first time in forever—in a long column of sexy gold. The color had looked great with her short, black hair. It had been a nice change from her usual jeans and shirt with her company dragonfly logo on it.

Ace had looked mouthwatering in his tuxedo. He'd lit up all her girly parts, and she'd had a few champagnes. She'd been dancing with some guy when Ace had swooped in, all dark and intense. That handsome, sharp face, the scruff on his jaw that drove her nuts, and dark hair long enough to tie back in a tiny ponytail.

He'd dragged her into a dark corner, all angry about her dancing with a stranger. He'd yelled, she'd yelled.

Then she'd had the startling realization that he was jealous.

Before she could process that, he'd kissed her.

Maggie pulled in a shuddering breath. Even now, she felt the tingles, the flush of heat.

She'd kissed him back. She'd let him drag her into a dark, private alcove at the gala and let him fuck her against the wall. It had been followed by a full night spent in his bed, doing more sexy, naughty things.

"Ms. Lopez?"

She jerked, yanked out of her thoughts by one of the scientists. She spotted the other two coming out of the trees, backpacks on, walking back toward the helo.

"Sorry. All done?" She dredged up a smile for Dr. Spiner.

"Yes," he clipped. "Let's go." He brushed past her.

Asshole. He'd been rude when they'd met this morning, too.

Shrugging, Maggie climbed into her helo and got Hetty prepped for the flight back to San Francisco.

The black Bell 407 LongRanger was her pride and joy. Hetty wasn't the latest model—there was no way Maggie could afford that—but Hetty got the job done. Maggie had a *long* way to go to get Hetty paid off, but Vander had helped her to secure the loan. Her business was growing, slowly but surely. There was also work doing aerial tours of San Francisco and the Bay, ferrying corporate bigwigs around, and doing aerial photography.

Her throat closed. How the hell could she make it all work with a baby?

She blew out a breath, then pulled her headset on. That was a worry for later.

Dr. Spiner sat in the back and roughly fastened his harness. He had a stony face, and well-cut, dark-brown hair. He'd probably be good-looking if he smiled. The other two climbed in—one tall with sandy-blond hair, the other shorter and stocky with black hair. As the men settled, she noticed the blond man's ass as he bent over. Weird. He'd struck her as a little overweight when they'd boarded this morning.

She looked up and saw Dr. Spiner eyeing her coldly.

Righto. She shook it off and spoke into her headset. "Everyone strap in, we'll be back in the city shortly."

She checked the instrument panel. Her gaze snagged on a small chain with a pretty dragonfly pendant hanging off it. She touched it. Ace had given it to her when she'd first started Dragonfly Aerial.

Letting the pendant go, she focused on the controls. Moments later, she talked to air traffic control and took off. As they moved over the water, she looked at the view.

It always made her blood pressure drop and a sense of wonder fill her. She loved San Francisco.

She'd grown up here. Her parents had since retired south to Monterey, but San Francisco would always be home.

They crossed just north of the Golden Gate Bridge, then over Alcatraz Island. Soon, the yacht marina and small pier beside it came into view. The pier was home to the landing pad where Dragonfly Aerial had its office and small hangar.

She swept in, hovered, and landed. She went through shutting down and saw her employee, Gus—a former Navy man—lumber out wearing his usual grease-stained coveralls. Gus kept his gray hair cut military short. She gave him a wave through the window. He'd take care of Hetty.

As she climbed out of the helicopter, she suddenly felt starving. She really wanted a doughnut with sprinkles.

"I hope you got everything you needed," she said to the scientists. They were all pulling their backpacks on.

"We did," Dr. Spiner clipped.

The other two men headed toward their car, parked on the other side of the chain-link fence. The blond guy was in way better shape than she'd realized. He reminded her of Ace's long, rangy body.

Looking back at Dr. Spiner's cold face, she tried for some professional courtesy. "Great. I got some excellent drone photography footage as well. So, it's a win-win."

The man stilled. "Drone photography?"

"Yes. Dragonfly Aerial specializes in both helicopter and drone photography, if you're ever interested."

He stepped closer, right into her personal space. "What did you take footage of?"

Maggie frowned and straightened. She was more than equipped to deal with assholes. "The scenery—"

He stepped even closer.

"Hey." She pressed a hand to his chest.

The man's blue eyes glittered. "I think you—"

Whatever he was going to say was lost in the throaty roar of a motorcycle.

They both looked up and watched a sleek, black bike sweep in. The suit and the helmet did nothing to hide the rider's muscular body.

The motorcycle stopped nearby, and the man set the kickstand down, then pulled his helmet off.

Vander Norcross's rugged face was easy to look at. His Italian-American heritage was obvious in his dark hair and good looks. But the scary, alert way he watched everything added an edge to the handsome man, and made people shiver.

As his dark gaze glanced at Maggie, then moved to Dr. Spiner, the scientist stepped back.

Maggie let out a breath. With a sharp nod, the man strode off.

"Hey, Vander." Maggie walked over to him.

The head of Norcross Security swung off his bike. "Was passing by. I wanted to check and make sure you were coming to the company party tonight at the Alchemist."

Damn, she'd been planning to avoid it, although she

loved the dim, trendy vibe at the bar. She wanted to avoid questions over why she wasn't drinking for a bit longer, and the slim possibility that she'd run into Ace. But as far as she knew, he was still in New Orleans working a cyber-security job.

She had to face him sooner or later. He had the right to know.

Her belly did a slow tumble. "Well, I—"

"It's compulsory." Vander raised a brow. "I know you've been working hard these last few weeks."

"I have loans to pay."

"You still deserve a night off, Lopez."

She blew out a breath. "Fine." She suspected no one ever said no to Vander.

He reached out and touched her cheek. "You okay, Maggie?"

He was former Ghost Ops—the top-secret, special forces team made up of the military's best of the best. It meant he saw too much.

She pasted on the bright smile. "Yep."

"Okay, see you tonight." He paused. "Oh, and Ace is back from the job in New Orleans. I'm sure he'll want to catch up with you, too."

Now her smile felt brittle. "Great. Sure. See you tonight."

ACE OLIVEIRA SIPPED HIS BEER, his gaze aimed at the door.

The Norcross Security party was in full swing.

Vander put on a couple of these shindigs each year. The Alchemist Bar wasn't far from the Norcross Security office in South Beach, with an industrial, steampunk décor, and good drinks. He liked the exposed-brick wall, the old-fashioned, leather armchairs, and all the brass accents.

Ace sipped again, and scanned the room. It was filled with Norcross Security employees and contractors, clients, and people's partners. Everyone was laughing and having a good time.

He wasn't. He felt edgy.

He'd been in New Orleans on a cyber-security job for almost two weeks, and before that, in New York for a few days to help Vander's friends—Maverick Rivera, Zane Roth, and Liam Kensington.

And before that, a certain leggy, smart-mouthed brunette had been dodging him. Maggie had been ignoring his calls, and conveniently missing him by a few minutes when he'd tried to track her down.

He took another sip, his fingers clenching on the glass bottle.

For the last few weeks, he'd had the taste of her in his mouth, he'd dreamed of those long legs wrapped tight around his hips, and his cock deep inside her. He knew just how tight she was. Knew the hungry sounds she made.

A part of him knew he should never have touched her, but he hadn't thought about that at the jewelry gala. That night, he hadn't been able to think through his need for her. That dress, that looked like liquid gold on her slim curves, had short-circuited his brain. Her short, dark hair had showed off her slim neck—the one vulnerable point on the feisty pilot who never showed any vulnerabilities. He'd wanted to kiss and bite it.

After the drama of the gala—where Rome had saved his princess from a stalker—Ace had taken Maggie home.

They hadn't slept. They'd fucked, again and again, until his bed was a shambles.

Every time he'd sunk inside her, he'd kept hoping the need for her would lessen.

He released a slow breath.

When he'd woken after that night, she'd been gone. Like a damn dream, except that her smell had still been on his sheets.

Even now, he felt a spurt of hot anger. He'd tried to call, track her down, but she'd avoided him. Then work had kept him away.

He was done.

He was not letting her fucking avoid him anymore.

Vander had told him that she was coming tonight, so Ace was going to pin her down and...

Fuck. He still wanted her. Under his hands. On his cock. In his bed.

Shit. Maggie was young, and his friend, and she worked for Norcross. It had messy written all over it. And Ace didn't do messy.

He looked up. He saw Rhys nuzzling his woman, Haven. Vander's younger brother was cross-eyed in love. Nearby, their sister Gia was arguing with her man, Saxon. Saxon worked for Norcross as well, and his arms were crossed over his chest as she waved hers around.

Suddenly, Saxon yanked her into his arms and ended the argument with a deep kiss.

"Hi, Ace."

He looked down at the curvaceous blonde in a form-fitting green dress. Harlow Carlson smiled up at him.

"Hey, Harlow." He didn't see Easton, but the oldest Norcross wouldn't be very far from his fiancée.

"How was New Orleans?" she asked.

"Steamy." He'd worked his ass off to get the job done a few days early and get home. He hadn't even been tempted to explore the nightlife.

"I bet that your brother missed you," Harlow said.

Ace smiled. "Yeah. I saw Rodrigo this morning." His younger brother had suffered a drug overdose the first time he'd tried drugs as a teenager, and it had left him with an acquired brain injury. He lived in a great care facility, and Ace visited him every week.

"How are you?" Ace asked Harlow.

She smiled. "Great. Easton is awesome, even when he drives me crazy."

The pair were living together, and she'd been his assistant. "Still working with him?"

"I'm back with my regular boss." Harlow smiled. "Easton seems to find a lot more reasons to visit Meredith these days." Harlow looked across the room. "And my parents are doing well."

Ace eyed the older couple. Harlow's father had gotten into debt with some bad people, and Harlow had been dragged into the mess until Easton had intervened.

Harlow made an annoyed sound and he followed her

gaze. A young boy, about eleven or so, was tugging on Vander's sleeve.

"I need to extract Daniel before he stomps on Vander's last nerve."

Ace grinned. Daniel was a street kid that Harlow's parents had taken in. He'd decided he wanted to work for Vander and took every opportunity to convince Vander to hire him. Harlow hurried off.

A sweet laugh filled the air, and Ace turned his head. Sofie didn't look much like a princess when she was snort-laughing over a cocktail. Rome sat on a curved bench seat beside her, his big body sprawled out, although Ace highly doubted that Rome was as relaxed as he looked. The man was always aware of the room, the people in it, the entrances and exits. It made him a damn good bodyguard. He was smiling at his woman as he reached out to toy with a strand of her strawberry-blonde hair.

"Hi, there."

Ace dragged his gaze away. A small, curvy blonde beamed up at him, wearing a clingy, blue top and tight jeans.

"Hi," he said.

"I'm friends with Amy. She's mentioned you. Said you're Brazilian."

Amy was an assistant who worked at the Norcross office.

"Yeah, I'm Ace."

"Jessica. It's a great party." She leaned into him and her flirty, floral perfume hit him. "Amy said you work with computers?"

"Yeah."

"I work in software implementation for finance." Her smile widened. "Probably *far* less interesting than security." She rested her hand on his forearm, the invitation obvious.

Something made him look up. He saw Maggie standing just inside the door of the bar, staring at him.

A jolt went through him. She wore wide-legged, black pants and a strapless red top that hugged her slim torso tightly. She had beautiful toned shoulders and arms.

Then her gaze dropped to Jessica pressing against his side.

Maggie's face hardened, then she swiveled and walked out.

Fuck.

He pushed away from Jessica and shoved through the crowd. He stormed out the door.

Maggie was walking down the sidewalk, past the outside tables packed with more customers, her long legs moving quickly.

"*Maggie.*"

She sped up.

Cursing, Ace ran after her. Catching her, he grabbed her arm and spun her around.

"Lopez, what the hell? You've been avoiding me for weeks. Why won't you even talk to me?"

Her chin jutted out. "It looked like you were busy."

"I was just being friendly."

She made a sound. "Friendly, right."

He leaned in. "Maggie, we need to talk."

God, this close, her spicy scent hit him—something

that made him think of vanilla and berries. It made him remember having her naked under him. His mouth traveling over all those places she'd dabbed with that scent.

A bus rumbled past and he heard loud laughter from the tables nearby, but he focused on Maggie's face. There was a watery gleam in her dark eyes. They were shades darker than his own brown eyes.

Shit. "Are you crying?"

"No." She pressed a hand to her mouth. "Fuck, I shouldn't have come."

Ace felt something close to panic. "Maggie, I don't want what we did to change anything. You're my friend."

Unreadable emotions flitted over her face. "*Friend.*" She gave a harsh laugh.

"Maggie?" He gripped her smooth shoulders. Crap. He wanted to stroke her skin, kiss the back of her neck.

"Things have already changed, Ace. We can't go back."

His gut clenched. "Maggie—"

She lifted her chin. "I'm pregnant."

CHAPTER TWO

Just looking at Ace made every part of Maggie light up and quiver.

Damn him for looking so good—sexy, edgy, with a smile made to seduce.

But that smile wasn't evident right now.

Her belly filled with flutters. Of course, she'd find him snuggled up with a cute, curvy blonde. The complete opposite of Maggie. She swallowed past the rock in her throat.

And now, she'd just blurted out the secret that she'd been holding onto for a week. She felt a bit sick.

He blinked. The man had ridiculously long lashes.

"What?" he said.

"I'm pregnant, Ace."

He cocked his head like he didn't quite trust his hearing. "You're fucking with me."

Anger spurted through her. She grabbed onto it—it was a safer emotion than any of the others. "No, Ace. We fucked. Repeatedly. Sometimes there are consequences."

He let her go and stepped back, sucking in a sharp breath.

It hurt. It hurt so much. There was disbelief in his eyes, and it was like a knife to her chest.

"We used condoms," he said carefully.

"We did, eventually. And as you should know, they're not one hundred percent. Besides, you didn't at first."

No, that first time had been a flash of passion in a dark hall at the gala. He'd thrust inside her bare, neither of them caring for a second. Then he'd recovered enough to suit up.

Apparently, too late.

His chest heaved. "Are you sure it's mine?"

Maggie gasped. The hurt arrowed so deep that she doubled over. *Damn him*. How could he hurt her so much?

He cursed and reached for her.

She stepped back, evading his hand.

"Maggie—" His tone changed, filled with regret.

"Don't touch me," she whispered, fighting back tears. *God*. "You're an asshole."

He put his hands on his hips, confusion and frustration on his handsome face. "Look—"

"I don't need anything from you." She lifted her chin. "You had a right to know, now you do. Stay away from me."

"Maggie." His voice firmed and he lunged for her.

She jerked back. "I said don't touch me."

"Everything okay?"

The dark, deep voice cut through the tension like a sword.

Maggie looked up to find Vander watching them like a hawk.

"Everything's fine." She needed to get away.

She turned, pushing through some people standing outside the bar, then ran back inside. She spotted the sign to the ladies' room, and dashed toward it.

She slammed into the restroom to find it mercifully empty.

Maggie splashed water on her face and pressed a hand to the sink. That had not gone well. *Dios mío.*

She felt tears again, but sucked them back. What good would tears do?

She'd learned that as a teenager, trying desperately to get her father's approval. She looked in the mirror, and saw the misery in her eyes.

What the hell was she going to do?

What you've always done. Take care of yourself. Prove everyone wrong and do what needed to be done.

The door opened, and she straightened like she'd been slapped.

Gia Norcross—petite, curvy, with waves of dark-brown curls, and a bossy look in her eyes— strode in, followed by Harlow, Sofie, and Haven.

Ambush. *Damn you, Vander.*

"Are you all right, Maggie?" Gia asked.

Maggie put on her trademark grin. "It's a party, of course I'm fine."

Gia sniffed. "I smell trouble. And I grew up with three brothers who could find trouble without even trying. Ladies, what do you think?"

"Man trouble," Harlow said.

"Hot, sexy guy trouble," Sofie said in her crisp, polished accent.

Damn. Maggie smoothed a hand over her hair. "Ace and I had a silly fight. Everything is fine. Nothing a gin and tonic won't fix." Maybe she could bribe the bartender to do a G and T without the G.

Haven stepped forward. "Maggie, all of us have recently been through some tough times. And also dealt with men who turned our worlds upside down."

"And inside out," Gia said dryly.

Maggie released a shuddering breath.

"We're here, Maggie." Harlow grabbed her hand. "I... detected something between you and Ace when I first met you."

"He's certainly very easy to look at," Sofie said with a small smile.

"He and I have always been friends," Maggie said. "He's Brazilian, my dad is Latino. We tease each other about the similarities and differences between Portuguese and Spanish."

Harlow cleared her throat. "He calls her *gatinha*. Kitten."

The women all made *ooh* sounds.

"He doesn't look at you like a friend," Harlow added.

"Really?" Maggie hated the catch in her chest.

Harlow nodded. "Really."

"I've had a thing for him for ages." Maggie shook her head. "I tried to talk myself out of it. He's very happy being an unattached man who's free to sample."

Gia tossed her head back. "That pretty much applied to all our men."

Maggie wrapped her arms around herself. "It doesn't matter. Everything is messed up."

"Honey." Harlow slid an arm around Maggie's waist. "You can tell us. We'll help."

"I'm pregnant." The words flew out of her.

There were several gasps of shocked surprise.

"Oh my," Sofie murmured.

"You're pregnant?" Gia said. "With Ace's baby?"

She nodded.

"And you just told him," Haven added.

Maggie gave a miserable nod. "I'd worked it all out in my head, but seeing him—" she swallowed "—I just blurted it out."

Gia took her hands and squeezed. "And I'm guessing he didn't take it very well. What did he say?"

"Was I sure it was his."

Now she got enraged gasps.

"He what?" Harlow snapped.

"What was he thinking?" Gia squeezed Maggie's fingers again.

Haven hugged her. Then they were all hugging her.

Tears pricked her eyes. Maggie had always been a tomboy, and then she'd joined the Navy. She was used to being around guys and having guys as friends. Not girl-friends.

The female solidarity surrounding her felt nice. She'd felt so alone the last few weeks. She hadn't even told her parents about the baby. They'd be supportive, but disappointed. She knew she wouldn't be able to face her father's repeated "I told you sos" just yet.

Gia patted her back. "That man."

Maggie saw Gia plotting.

"Now, not to defend him," Sofie said. "But it was probably a shock."

Haven's nose wrinkled. "How long have you known, Maggie?"

"A week."

"You've had some time to process and adjust," Haven said quietly.

"Have you seen a doctor yet?" Sofie asked.

Maggie nodded. "She confirmed I'm pregnant and took some blood. She gave me a prenatal vitamin."

"Give Ace some time." Gia hugged Maggie. "Now, I'm going to get Saxon to drive you home."

"No, I—"

"Yes. No arguments."

Gia Norcross wasn't a woman to take no for an answer.

Maggie gave in and let them take care of her.

FUCK. *Fuck.*

Ace ran his hands through his hair, tearing the band loose.

Maggie was *pregnant.*

His mind shied away from the thought. He paced the dark corner of the bar. Part of him wanted to find her.

The hurt on her face had slayed him. He'd opened his mouth before his brain had taken a chance to compute.

Fuck.

"Ace?"

Easton appeared. The man's face was serious and worried.

Ace's heart thumped. "You know?"

"I know something went down. Harlow asked me to check on you."

Ace blew out a breath. "I need to talk to Maggie."

"Saxon and Gia are dropping her off at home."

"Dammit." He spun, trying to work through everything. He couldn't breathe.

"Come on." Easton jerked his head. "I'll buy you a drink."

With nothing else to do, Ace followed Easton.

The oldest Norcross brother ordered two scotches on the rocks. Ace leaned against the bar and took a hefty gulp.

Across the room, Vander was talking with a few clients. He glanced over a few times, his brow creased.

Shit. Ace would have to tell Vander, and his boss would be pissed. He treated Maggie like a sister. All the guys did.

Except Ace had never looked at Maggie like a sister. He'd tried to and failed.

He took another gulp of his drink. He felt Easton's gaze.

"You want to talk about it?"

"Shit, Easton." Ace set the glass on the bar. "Maggie's pregnant."

Easton's brows shot up. He took a slow sip of his own drink. "And you're the father?"

Father. How the hell could he be a father? He'd never

wanted kids. He came from a shitty gene pool, and the one time he'd been left in charge of someone... Rodrigo had never been the same again.

Guilt washed over Ace—hot, sticky, all-too-familiar. He hadn't protected his brother.

But that wasn't even the worst of it. What was in his blood was far, far worse.

How the hell could he protect and care for a child?

He cleared his throat. "Yes."

"Ace, Jesus." Easton dragged in a breath. "What are you planning to do?"

"I don't know. Maggie just told me, and I reacted badly."

"Ah."

"I fucked up, Easton."

"Well you better un-fuck it, or Vander will make you regret it."

Ace blew out a breath. "God, I've really screwed up. Maggie's young. In her twenties. And I've got no business being anyone's father. *Fuck*."

"Hey." Easton gripped Ace's shoulder. "There are two of you in this, and Maggie is not a child."

"I... Need some time, and I need to talk to Maggie."

Easton nodded. "Take the night. This is big news."

Ace slipped out of the party and pulled out his phone. He thumbed the button. He'd saved her under *gatinha*, his nickname for her.

Kitten. Because she liked birds, albeit large, metal ones with rotors.

The phone rang. And rang.

"Leave a message," Maggie's cheerful voice said.

22

"Maggie... Fuck, I'm sorry. You shocked me. I... We need to talk. Call me, *gatinha*. Please."

After he'd finished his drink, Ace slipped out of the bar and ordered an Uber. He headed back to his place in Buena Vista.

He'd owned an apartment in the city for a few years, but a year ago, he'd sold it and made a tidy profit. He'd decided it was time to buy a house.

He thanked the Uber driver and walked up the steps to his front door. Lights clicked on automatically. He thumbed his phone and turned off his alarm system.

Damn, he really wanted to see Maggie. He wanted to rewind and start again.

Hell, she was pregnant.

He stood in the entry of his house, staring at the wall. He didn't see the painting hanging there, his thoughts all turned inward.

They'd made a baby.

He felt faint prickles of panic. He headed up the stairs, assaulted by the memory of fucking Maggie on them.

His cock hardened.

He stomped into the living room.

She was right. The first time he'd had her, pinned against the wall at the gala, he'd been too far gone, too lost in his need for her. In a desperate hurry, he'd done something he'd never done in his entire life, and thrust into her bare.

Idiot. They'd both groaned, both felt how good it was.

It had brought him to his senses and he'd taken a second to get a condom out of his wallet and fucked her

THE HACKER

until she cried out. He captured her scream with his mouth.

Deus. He closed his eyes and dropped onto the couch. He'd fucked up. They needed to talk and sort things out. *Merda.*

He scraped a hand through his hair.

He and Maggie had made a baby. He stared out the huge windows. He had a kickass view of Corona Heights Park and the southern sprawl of San Francisco, although at night, it was just a spread of lights.

He tried to imagine a child fitting into their lives, but couldn't.

He pulled out his phone to text Maggie.

I'm thinking of you. We need to talk. I'm here for you.

He had no idea how he'd fall asleep. Instead, he went into his kitchen and pulled out his bottle of cachaça. He didn't bother with a glass. He sat, drank, and watched the lights of the city deep into the night.

CHAPTER THREE

F eeling a little queasy, Maggie strode into her small kitchen. She put some bread in the toaster and leaned against the counter.

Her torn-up bed told the story of her restless night. She kept seeing the shocked look in Ace's eyes, hearing his voice.

Are you sure it's mine?

Asshole. She yanked the fridge open, and pulled out some orange juice. She took a sip and paused. Her stomach swirled unhappily. Was this morning sickness starting or was she just feeling crapola?

The toast popped up and she slathered it with butter and honey. Then she grabbed her phone and pulled a face. She had a bunch of messages from Ace.

Her stomach whirled again. There were several voicemails, too. She deleted them without listening to them.

"You can jump in the Bay, Ace Oliveira." She

couldn't deal with him right now. She'd told him, now she could move on and deal with things by herself.

So, he thought she'd sleep around, then tell him he was going to be a father without being certain? He *knew* her. How the hell could he accuse her of that?

Maybe there was something wrong with her? It seemed like the men in her life always let her down.

She munched on the toast and looked out the window. She had a small apartment in the Marina District, close to work. The building was old, and her apartment was a cozy, one-bedroom. It wasn't fancy, since she funneled all her money into her business, but it did have warm, honey-colored wooden floors, which she loved.

This is crazy, Magdalena. You'll never make this business work. You'll just end up in debt. You'll be a failure.

Her father's voice. She sighed. Leo Lopez loved her. She was his only child, but he'd been a successful businessman with a fleet of small planes before he retired. He put a lot of expectation onto his only child.

He hadn't wanted her to join the Navy, hadn't wanted her to start her own business, wanted her to get married. He was always doubting her.

Like Ace had.

When her father finds out she is pregnant... *Ugh*. She finished the toast and pulled on her windbreaker and boots.

She needed to get to work. All the men in her life could take a flying leap.

She was taking Hetty out later this afternoon. Gus was

coming to help with maintenance. And this morning, she needed to put her new drone up for a test flight. She'd get some morning shots of the Golden Gate Bridge. She had another young employee, Charlie, who was her drone guy. He was twenty-two and a geek down to his bone marrow. He did a lot of her drone work, but he was currently in Australia on a two-month trip, getting drone footage of the outback.

That meant more work for Maggie.

As for Ace Oliveira, she was putting him in a box and not thinking about him for a while.

She jumped in her ancient, green Jeep and drove to the helipad and office. On days when she didn't have any gear and the weather was decent, she often walked. The rent for her office and helipad on the pier was exorbitant, but it was so worth it. Tourists and businesspeople made up the bulk of her clients.

She pulled to a stop in her allocated parking space outside the chain-link fence, and jumped out. The fog was burning off the Bay, and off to the left, she took a second to admire the Golden Gate Bridge. The view never got old.

She strode down the pier and unlocked the office. It wasn't much—the front room of the small building had a couch and some waiting chairs. Her desk was tucked into one corner, and there was a pocket-sized kitchen and bathroom.

Maggie filled the coffee machine and set it to work. The smell made her stomach curl up. She pressed a hand to her belly. She still couldn't quite comprehend that there was a life growing inside her.

She heard heavy footsteps and shook her head. She watched Gus stomp in.

"Morning," she said.

He grunted at her. Maggie grinned. She loved the old guy. She poured him a coffee and handed it to him. The chipped mug had "I'm not a superhero, but I'm a mechanic, so close enough" written on the front of it.

He grunted again, looked at the mug and shot her a look. "You think you're funny, girlie?"

"Yep." Since her stomach was still unhappy, she decided to forego her usual mug of coffee. "All the time."

"Cheeky. No respect."

She grinned at him. "Let's get to work on Hetty, old man."

Gus' gaze narrowed. "You look tired."

"Oh, you're so charming, and good for a woman's self-esteem." She shrugged a shoulder. "I didn't sleep well."

Her cell phone rang. The ring tone was a funky salsa song that she'd saved for Ace. Jaw hardening, she ended the call without accepting it.

Gus raised a brow. "That guy still causing you problems?"

It took her a second. "Chris? No." He was a guy she'd gone on a few dates with, who wasn't happy when she said she didn't want to see him anymore. They'd had zero chemistry, and the fact that she was obsessed with someone else didn't help. She lifted her chin. "He hasn't called in a while. This is something else. It's fine."

Gus didn't look convinced. "Need me to warn some other guy off?"

Warmth filled her chest, then she felt the dreaded

prickle behind her eyes. *Shit*. If she cried, Gus would be horrified. She was totally blaming hormones.

"Aww, look at you being sweet."

He sipped his coffee and shot her a look. "Let's get to work on that bird."

Maggie spent an hour with Gus, helping him with Hetty. Then she washed the grease off her hands and pulled out her new drone.

Her phone pinged. She glanced at the screen. More missed calls from Ace. She felt the temptation to answer, even as she told herself not to give in.

He'd made his feelings known. She just wanted to get on with her life. She huffed out a breath and snatched up the phone.

Answer the phone, gatinha. *I'm at work, but we need to talk.*

Please pick up.

Maggie, quit being stubborn. I said I was sorry.

He had? She wrinkled her nose. What was there to talk about? They'd had sex. She was pregnant. She couldn't see Ace settling down into domestic bliss, and she had no desire to watch him move onto the next pretty, young thing that caught his eye.

She couldn't afford to let him in. He'd walk away eventually.

Enough. Pick up the damn phone.

Mmm, someone was losing patience. Well, he'd have to wait until she was ready.

She opened the drone box. "Ooh."

The DJI Inspire 2 was pretty. Her older DJI Phantom 4 was great, but with this baby and its increased capabilities, she could take better photos, and make more money. Soon she'd have a little person to support, so this would help.

She pressed a palm to her belly, emotion swelling inside her.

She hadn't thought much past the shock and panic and surprise. Past the worry of telling Ace and her parents.

But she realized she wanted this child. It hadn't been planned, and she'd likely be doing this alone, but she'd never see it as a mistake. She wasn't a teenager, she was healthy, and she had a business.

There was no other option except to bring this little person into the world.

Maggie pulled the drone out and checked it over. She slipped her tablet into the controller, then grabbed everything, and headed outside. She set it down and went through the pre-start sequence.

She heard childish laughter and looked up. Through the fence, she saw a group of kids laughing as they walked past. Two women were with them, sipping coffees and chatting as the kids pointed at things, eyeing the boats in the marina next door.

Then her gaze snagged on a lone man at the fence. He had a ball cap pulled low over his face. He might have been looking at the boats, but Maggie got the distinct impression he was looking her way.

Probably admiring Hetty. Shaking her head, she started up the drone and clutched the tablet. The familiar whirr filled her ears. She sent the drone straight up, and then over the water.

Saturdays got pretty busy in the air around the Golden Gate Bridge and over the Bay. There were often lots of tour helicopters. Keeping a tight flight path, she flew out toward the bridge, zooming in to get some good shots.

The drone handled well. She did another loop, then sent it home.

She glanced over at the helo. Gus was busy with Hetty, and she could just see the bottom half of his body sticking out the back of the bird.

Maggie returned her gaze to the sky and quickly spotted the drone. Yep, it handled like a dream.

The kids were inside the fence now, at the edge of the water, pointing down at something.

She smiled. God, she was going to have a curious, laughing child before she knew it.

She lifted her head. The man at the fence had moved farther away, and it looked like he was hunched over his phone.

Suddenly, her tablet screen flickered.

Maggie frowned. *What the hell?*

It flickered again. She glanced up and saw the drone wobble.

Her heart shot into her throat. She hit the emergency home option. It should land automatically at her feet.

As she watched, the drone veered. It was falling like a bullet. Maggie tapped the screen again. Nothing.

Fuck. She set the controller down and lifted an arm to shield her eyes from sunlight.

Come on. Land.

The drone zigged and zagged, looking like it was drunk. *Shit*. It wasn't going to land like she'd hoped.

Then it sliced left—

Toward the kids.

Fuck. She sprinted forward. "Look out!"

The kids looked up, confused. The mothers frowned at her.

Maggie waved and pointed in the air.

The mothers dropped their coffee cups and jerked, launching at their kids.

"Come on." Maggie reached them, shoving them out of the way. "Get behind the fence."

They ran ahead of her, and Maggie spun. The drone aimed right at her.

She sprinted across the concrete toward her office.

The drone changed direction, arrowing toward her.

If it hit her...

It was going to hurt, or worse.

Maggie picked up speed, her lungs burning, her pulse racing.

All of a sudden, a heavy weight hit her legs and she crashed to the ground.

The drone flew overhead, close enough to touch, then smashed into the concrete with a deafening crunch.

———

ACE'S HEART was thumping hard as he kept Maggie pinned to the ground.

"You okay?" he asked.

"Ace?" She looked back over her shoulder, her voice breathless.

"Stay down." He pushed to his feet, eyeing the crashed drone. The rotors were still spinning and he kicked it, then again until the rotors stopped.

When he'd arrived, he'd seen the drone chasing Maggie and almost lost his shit.

His only thought was to get her safe.

He moved back to her. She stood up, her hands shaking a little.

He scanned her. She looked okay. He took a second to eye her flat belly and his throat tightened. "Are you hurt?"

"No. I don't—" She broke off and wavered on her feet.

Fucking hell. He scooped her up, holding her tight against his chest, and carried her toward the office. He saw her crusty mechanic striding over.

"What the hell happened with the new drone?" Gus barked.

"I don't know," she said.

Maggie leaned her head against Ace's chest and his heart thumped. He loved the feel of her in his arms.

"The drone just went crazy. The screen flickered, and it was like it suddenly had a mind of its own."

"I'll pick up the parts," Gus said, scowling.

Inside the dingy office, Ace set her down on the couch. He frowned. "It sounds like it got hacked."

She sucked in a breath. "Hacked? Why would someone hack my drone?"

"Because they can." Ace ran a hand up her leg.

She jerked. "Hey."

"Just checking you're okay." He pressed the other hand to the back of her neck and stroked the long line of it. She shivered and her gaze dropped. She had long, inky eyelashes.

"I'm fine," she said. "I just need to adjust to no coffee in the mornings."

Ace slid his hand down her arm, then hesitated. He pressed a hand to her belly.

She sucked in a breath and her gaze locked with his.

Then she surged up. "I need—"

"No." He grabbed her hand. "Maggie."

"You can't do this," she whispered. "I—"

"I'm sorry. I was shocked when you told me. I was an asshole."

She sat back against the couch. "A colossal asshole."

"Yes." Gently, he touched her belly again, spreading his fingers out. "I know you, and I know if you say it's mine, then it is."

"I haven't been with anybody else." She looked away.

"I haven't either." She'd been all he could think about.

Her head jerked and she made a sound of disbelief. "You were celibate while you were away in New York and New Orleans. Sure."

He gripped her chin and forced her to look at him. "I was working. And trying to get in touch with you. Thinking about you." He stroked her jaw. "Dreaming about you."

Liquid-brown eyes met his.

"Stroking my cock while thinking about you."

Her lips parted. "*Ace.*"

"You snuck out of my damn bed, Maggie. I was pissed. Then you avoided me."

She shifted. "I wanted to avoid the awkward, morning-after thing."

"And I wanted to fuck you in my shower and feed you breakfast." He cupped her cheek. "Can we start again? And discuss the situation?"

"It's a baby, Ace, not a situation."

He blew out a breath. A poor baby lumped with him for a father. "Right. Now, are you sure you're okay?"

She nodded. "I'm fine."

"Dinner. Tonight. My place."

She shook her head. "No—"

"Yes."

"*Ace.*"

"Dinner. Tonight."

She huffed out a breath. "Fine."

"Good." He felt a spurt of satisfaction. Because he needed it, he yanked her into his arms. She held herself stiffly, but he pressed his face to her hair and breathed her in. She always had a faint smell of jet fuel to her, but he liked it, especially mixed with that vanilla-berry scent of hers.

He ran a hand down her slim back.

"Right." He reluctantly pulled back. "I'm going to take a look at your drone."

She shot to her feet. "I want to see. I'll have to claim it on warranty."

He wanted her to rest, but the determined look on her face was one he knew all too well. There was no changing Magdalena Lopez's mind when she was determined to do something.

Gus had collected the ruined drone and controller and left it sitting outside the office door.

Ace crouched and lifted the controller. He pulled the tablet free and connected it to his phone.

He ran a little program he'd created. He'd spent several years at the National Security Agency—as part of their top-secret Red Team of the most-skilled hackers—and had loved computers from the day his father had let him play on his laptop. They sang for him.

He saw data flash on the screen and growled. "Definitely hacked."

Maggie blew out a breath and ran a hand through her hair. "I don't understand. Why the hell would someone do this?"

"There are all kinds of hackers. Some do it for the thrill, others for less-benign reasons."

"It must've been kids. And it got away from them."

Ace rose. He could see she wanted to believe that, but he'd seen the drone. It had been aiming for Maggie.

"How close would they need to be?" she asked.

"My guess is close."

She frowned, a groove on her brow. "There was a guy here—"

Now Ace frowned. "Guy? What guy?"

She shrugged. "I don't know. A tall guy by the fence. He was wearing jeans and a ball cap. He can't have been involved."

Ace scanned the now-empty fence line.

She shook her head. "It was just a stupid accident, Ace."

"Have you got problems with anyone?"

"No." She shook her head. "I try to make sure my customers are all happy. I pay my bills on time."

"Okay." He touched her again, and stroked her arm.

Her gaze met his and they stared at each other, and he felt the throb of connection. He wanted to kiss her.

She tugged away.

Tonight. He'd have her at his place and all to himself.

"Can I take this?" He held up the tablet.

"Yes, but I need it back." She suddenly looked tired and rubbed her forehead. "And now I need to call the manufacturer and yell at them. My expensive drone is in bits and I want a new one."

Ace smiled. "I'm pretty sure they'll cave under the wrath of Magdalena Lopez."

"Don't call me Magdalena." She shot him a disgruntled look.

He kissed her nose. "It's a pretty name."

"I know. It doesn't suit me."

"You're pretty." He lowered his voice. "Pretty breasts, pretty nipples, pretty pussy—"

She sucked in a breath and tried to smack him. "Ace!"

He caught her hand. "I'll see you tonight, *gatinha*."

She nodded.

Ace headed back to his car, and looked at the tablet in his hands. He'd run some tests back in his computer lab.

Maggie was his to protect.

CHAPTER FOUR

Maggie found a parking spot just down from Ace's house in Buena Vista. His place was nestled between Buena Vista Park and Corona Heights Park.

The night she'd been here, she'd had a few drinks and had been so wrapped up in Ace that she hadn't really paid much attention to his house.

Walking down the steep street, a faint, uneasy feeling welled up inside of her. It was a grown-up street, with nice, grown-up houses.

She had a crappy apartment. The same place she'd lived in since she'd gotten out of the Navy.

She paused in front of his place.

Shit. It was nice. *Really* nice.

It looked modern and architectural. It was covered in redwood siding, with long, sleek windows, and black, metal accents. She was sure it had cost a pretty penny.

Vander paid well, and his brother Easton was a billionaire businessman. She knew that Easton helped the Norcross guys invest, and he'd given her some pointers, too.

She looked down at her shoes. She was wearing flats and jeans. She'd changed five times tonight, cycling through jeans, pants, a skirt, and back to jeans. She wore her favorite dark jeans, a cute blouse, a nice, navy-blue blazer and a pretty, emerald-green scarf. She didn't belong in this fancy house. Maybe she should've dressed up, after all.

Up the set of metal stairs, the front door opened, and Ace stood there in jeans that fit his sexy body, and a tight, gray Henley. His hair was out, brushing his shoulders.

Heat pooled in her belly. She loved his hair. It was sexy as hell tied back, and even sexier loose.

"Are you just going to stand there on the sidewalk?" he asked.

She scratched her ear. "Maybe."

"Don't you like my place?"

"I like it too much. It's a grown-up house."

"I am older than you."

She scoffed and walked up the stairs. "Yes, you're ancient. Seven years is a huge gap, Oliveira." She stopped in front of him.

"Hey," he said quietly.

"Hey."

He took her hand and pulled her inside. His feet were bare, and she found that sexy as hell.

No, no finding him sexy. She was here to discuss the baby, and that was it. Maggie couldn't afford to get sucked back into Ace's vortex. She had enough to deal with without dealing with a broken heart.

Her gaze dropped to his ass and she stifled a groan. She was blaming the baby hormones.

He towed her up some interior stairs. Color hit her cheeks because she remembered exactly what they'd done on that staircase.

She looked around the open plan living, dining, and kitchen areas. The floors were a warm wood, and he had a funky-patterned, black-and-white rug under the long couch. A wooden table was set against one wall, with the cute kitchen at the back. It had a white island, white cabinets, some cool open shelving, and a fun, patterned, gray-tile backsplash. But as she turned, it was the huge floor to ceiling windows and the view beyond that caught the eye.

The city sprawled down the valley and, in the distance, she saw the water. *Wow.*

She looked back into the living room, and her gaze snagged on the bold art on the walls.

Huge paintings hung on several walls. One was large with interesting textures that made her think of trees. Another was a wild explosion of color and shapes.

"You collect art?" she asked.

He circled the island. "You sound surprised."

"I guess I expected you to have keyboards or monitors on the wall."

His lips quirked. "I'm not all techie, you know."

Oh, she knew that. She had the positive pregnancy test to prove it.

"I like collecting art." He nodded at the colorful painting. "That's by an up-and-coming, young, Brazilian artist."

Maggie had a Funko Pop figure of a Star Wars Rebel pilot a friend had given her. That was about the extent of her art collection

"Drink?" He paused. "Nothing alcoholic, of course." He had a bottle of Anchor Stream beer open.

"Sparkling water."

"On it."

The smell of something delicious hit her. "You're cooking?"

"I hear more surprise in your voice, *gatinha*." He poured some San Pellegrino into a glass with ice. "I can cook."

Her uncomfortable feeling grew. She realized she didn't really know him as well as she thought.

"I'm making *caldinho de feijão*. A good, tasty Brazilian black bean soup. It's my father's recipe."

Maggie sat on the stool and sipped her drink. "Your father cooks?"

"Yup. *Minha mãe* is very bad in the kitchen. She tries and fails miserably." A fond smile hit his face. "We all pretend to like it."

Maggie snorted. "My father only steps into the kitchen to mix drinks. He believes it's a woman's domain. My mother does all the cooking."

Ace eyed her. "He's traditional?"

Another snort escaped. "More like a little rigid. Women should get married and have babies." She wrinkled her nose. "They shouldn't join the Navy, or start their own business."

Ace frowned. "I take it you haven't told him that you're pregnant?"

She shook her head. "I wanted to tell you first. Maybe come up with a plan for how I was going to deal with work and a baby."

He reached for her hand. "I am sorry I really reacted badly."

She sighed. "I hadn't intended to spring it on you the way I did. It just blurted out. I've had a week to adjust to it, and I'll admit I'm still a bit freaked out."

"But you want the baby?"

She nodded, throat tight.

"I never thought much about kids," he said. "Mostly had nothing to do with them, except distant kids of cousins." He shrugged. "I'm not sure I'm a good option for a dad."

There was something in his eyes. A real pain. What the hell was he talking about? Ace was a smart, decent guy.

"And you really want this baby, Maggie?"

She swallowed and looked at his serious face. "Yes. I...can't even comprehend other options. I'm not too young. My business isn't as established as I would like, but yes, I want this baby."

He nodded. "Then we'll work it out."

She bit her lip, a confusing tangle of emotions inside her.

An alarm beeped, and he turned to the simmering pan on the stove. "Dinner's ready. We can eat on the roof deck."

"You have a roof deck?" She watched him scoop the thick soup into two bowls, then garnish it with fried bacon and parsley.

"It's what sold me on the place. I bought the house a year ago. I was ready for a change from apartment living. This place was built by an architect and his husband, but they were leaving town, so I got a good deal." He nodded his head. "Grab the drinks."

They went up some stairs and stepped out into the brisk night air.

Maggie sucked in a breath. Oh, she loved this.

The deck was all redwood with iron railings, but the sweeping view of the city was beyond incredible. There was a wooden table set up with a brazier burning nearby. Ace set the bowls down.

"Eat." He waved a hand.

She sat across from him. They ate, keeping talk to work and other light topics. The soup—filled with blended black beans and bacon—was great.

"Hopefully I won't come down with food poisoning tomorrow," she teased.

He kicked her under the table.

Maggie swallowed a spoonful of soup. "Or morning sickness. I was a bit queasy this morning."

He froze with his spoon half way to his mouth.

Her stomach lurched. "Sorry. I shouldn't have that brought up."

He grabbed her hand. "You're not alone. I just need a bit more time to get my head around it all. We'll work things out."

She nodded. Topic change. "Did you find anything on my drone?"

His face hardened. "I'm running some more tests. It

was definitely hacked, but I don't know by whom, or why."

"I'm guessing that's nearly impossible to work out, especially if it was just kids."

He made a sound.

She cocked her head. "Did I just insult the great Ace Oliveira?"

"I have some tricks up my sleeve."

They finished the meal, and he led her over to a built-in wooden bench.

There were some blankets folded nearby and he wrapped one around her. The lights of the city twinkled like jewels.

This was a little too cozy. She needed to keep things businesslike between them. She couldn't afford to get lulled by romantic rooftop views, or his damn sexy cologne.

"Warm enough?" he asked.

"Yes." Her gaze snagged on his shadowed face. His lips were full and sexy, and she loved them. Loved what they could do.

"Maggie, if you keep looking at my mouth like that..."

"I'm not." She turned her head, staring blindly at the view.

He grabbed her hand and pulled it up to his stubbled jaw.

"Ace—"

"Missed you. So damn much."

Her heart lurched in her chest. "Look, now more than ever we need to keep things friendly and—"

He sucked her finger into his mouth and everything

inside her pulsed. She wrestled with a rush of desire. "Ace, we aren't doing this." Her voice was a little husky.

He shifted closer. "That's the way you murmured my name when I slid inside you."

She whimpered.

Then he pulled her close and pressed his mouth to hers.

No. Yes. Everything inside her struggled. Getting too close to this man was bad for her.

The hell with it. Maggie threw her arms around his neck and kissed him back.

MAGGIE WAS IN HIS ARMS, kissing him.

Right where he wanted her.

Desire surged through Ace and he leaned over her, pushing her back on the bench. He plunged his tongue into her mouth, cupping the back of her head.

Her fingers shoved into his hair and she moaned into his mouth. She undulated against him, wrapping one long leg around his hip. She rubbed against his rock-hard cock, making him fight back a groan.

That's what he remembered most. Maggie was highly sexual, letting it all loose as they'd loved each other. She touched and kissed him like she'd never get enough. Hell, she'd sucked his cock like she'd enjoyed it more than he had—and he'd fucking loved it.

She made a hungry sound and he deepened the kiss. When she rubbed against him again, he thought his cock might break, or that he might come in his jeans—something he hadn't ever done.

"*Ace,*" she breathed, her tone soaked in need.

"I know, *gatinha.*" He slid a hand between them and rubbed along the seam of her jeans.

She sucked on his tongue and the kiss turned wilder. He kept rubbing, wanting her naked, but he couldn't do that out here. And he didn't want to break the moment.

The ringing of a cell phone cut through the night. Ace cursed.

"Shit." She shoved against him. He watched panic flood her eyes, and she pushed against his chest. "Off."

Dammit. "Maggie—"

"We *aren't* doing this, Ace."

"Yes, we are," he growled.

She shook her head, and Ace desperately wanted to kiss her again, but the phone kept ringing.

He muttered a curse. "That's Vander's ringtone."

She made a sound and dropped back. Ace took a second to look at her face. She wasn't conventionally beautiful, but she was striking, with her pointed chin and liquid-dark eyes.

He rose and made no effort to hide his raging hard-on. Her gaze dropped, and even in the dim lighting, he could tell she was blushing.

He grabbed his cell phone. "Yeah."

There was a pause. "I'm interrupting?" Vander asked.

"I'm guessing you wouldn't be calling on a Saturday night if it wasn't important."

"Yeah. Saxon and I are doing a small, last-minute job

tonight. I need you to run some intel and handle comms for me."

Ace blew out a breath. "Okay. I'll get on it. Send me the details and I'll get some searches running. Then I need to drop someone home and I'll be on the job."

Vander cursed. "Didn't know you had company."

"It's okay. Work is work. I won't leave you and Saxon hanging."

"Thanks, Ace."

This might help buy him some points for when Vander found out what was going down with him and Maggie.

He met her gaze. She'd risen, her body stiff, and he could see she was rebuilding that prickly shell of hers.

Oh, no, gatinha, I'm not letting you run away from me again. "I need—"

She nodded. "I heard. And I have my Jeep, so no need to drop me home."

They headed back inside.

"Let me grab some shoes." He flicked on the TV. "I just need a few minutes in my office to set some searches running."

"I can—"

"I'm walking you to your car, Maggie. And fair warning, I'm kissing you again."

Her chin jerked up. "No kissing. That was a mistake."

Cute. He'd never guessed sharp-edged Maggie Lopez could be cute.

"We'll see." He strode into his home office. Ace checked his computer, found the email from Vander, and set up the searches. Then he stopped in his bedroom to grab some shoes and a jacket.

Back in the living room, Maggie was watching the news. When she saw him, she rose from the couch, then her head whipped around to the TV.

"—body found in the Muir Woods National Monument today. The victim had been murdered, although police aren't providing any details. The victim has been identified as Adrian Marks of Portola. Mr. Marks was a city building inspector."

The man's picture blinked up on screen. Blond, ordinary-looking, maybe forty-five.

Maggie gasped.

"Maggie?" Ace stepped closer. She'd turned as white as a sheet. "Maggie?" He helped her sit on the arm of his couch. "Do you know that guy?"

"I don't know." She shook her head. "He looks a little like one of the scientists I took out to Muir Woods yesterday." She shook her head. "But I flew all three of them back, very much alive."

"So, it can't be one of your clients."

"Right." Her brow furrowed and she stared at the screen until the story changed. "And they were scientists studying the redwoods, not building inspectors." She shook her head and rose. "Okay, I'll go so you can help out the boss man."

Ace walked her to her ancient green Jeep, then pinned her against it, now reluctant to let her leave.

"Oliveira." She shoved against him.

He didn't budge. "I want to see you tomorrow. We can talk more." He rubbed his nose against hers.

Her body trembled. "We aren't getting involved, Ace. We have enough complications to deal with."

"Okay."

She eyed him suspiciously.

"But we do need to talk. Come over for lunch tomorrow."

"You might have a late night."

"I'll text you in the morning. I'll probably need to debrief with Vander, but I'll keep you posted."

She nodded.

Then he leaned in. He felt her stiffen, just as he closed his mouth over hers. Just like that, need hit him in the gut. He opened his mouth and her head dropped back. Her hands slid up his back. He swallowed her moan and they clung to each other, going at it against her Jeep.

When he lifted his head, they were both panting.

"I said no kissing," she murmured. Her cheeks were flushed.

"No, you didn't. Fuck, I don't want to let you go."

She licked her lips, and she looked like she was fighting some internal battle.

With a groan, he kissed her again. He slid his hands to her denim clad ass and gave it a squeeze.

It took one second before she was responding, her tongue sliding against his.

Ace lifted his head. "Go. Another second and I'll be dragging you inside."

"No, you wouldn't, because we *aren't* doing this. No kissing, no touching."

He just smiled at her.

She scowled and pulled in a breath. "Thanks for dinner."

She opened the door of her Jeep and slid inside. He leaned in through the open door. "Drive safely, and text me when you get home."

She rolled her eyes. "I'm a big girl, Oliveira. I've been driving myself around for years."

"Yeah, well, I can still taste your lips and you're pregnant."

Her gaze flew up to his, and the air charged. He realized it was the first time he'd brought it up himself. His gut churned.

"Text me," he said.

"All right."

"Night, *gatinha.*"

"Night, Ace."

He watched her drive away until her brake lights disappeared from view.

He still wasn't on an even keel about this pregnancy, but he wanted Maggie. She'd be here tomorrow and they'd sort some things out.

For now, he headed inside to call Vander.

CHAPTER FIVE

Maggie headed up the stairs to her apartment.
What had she been thinking? She wasn't
supposed to be kissing Ace. She nibbled on her bottom
lip. She was supposed to be acting like an adult, not
indulging in more of the same behavior that had gotten
her into this situation.

"Not that you're a situation." She patted her belly.

Dinner had been nice. She loved his place. And
clearly pregnancy hadn't dimmed the desire she felt
for him.

She pinched the bridge of her nose. She couldn't
sleep with him again. If she got involved like that…
Maggie knew she'd fall for him. Totally. And one day,
he'd decide the footloose and fancy-free lifestyle he'd led,
filled with hot, single women, was much more exciting
than her and a child.

At least Ace seemed to be sort-of coming around to
the idea of the pregnancy. They hadn't talked too much

about the details, but she was cautiously hopeful he'd help.

She was almost to her front door when she saw it was ajar. Her heart stopped. *Oh, no.*

Frozen to the spot, she wasn't sure what to do. Run and get help? Call the police? She stepped closer and didn't hear anything from inside.

Her fingers slid into her pocket and curled around her phone. Her first instinct was to call Ace.

Maggie swallowed. *No.* She'd just lectured herself on not getting more entwined with him than she needed to be. She was a big girl, and she was used to dealing with things by herself.

Swiveling, she walked to her neighbor's door and knocked.

A second later, the strong, square-jawed face of Hank Paulson appeared. "Hey, Maggie."

"Hi, Hank." He was a short, stocky man with dark skin and a bald head. He and his wife had twin sons who were the lights of their life. Since Maggie didn't hear any noise from inside, she assumed the boys were asleep. Twin five-year-old boys were *not* quiet. "Um, I think someone broke into my place."

Frowning, he stepped into the corridor and looked at her open door. "Aw, hell."

"Pretty sure they're gone, but can you check with me?"

"You called the police?"

"Not yet, but I will."

"Hang on a sec." He ducked back into his place and reappeared with a baseball bat.

The two of them approached her apartment.

Hank nudged the door open. The place looked untouched. A part of her had been expecting a mess.

Heart thumping hard, she flicked on the light.

Hank moved inside. "Stay behind me."

Quickly, they checked the bedroom and bathroom. There was no one hiding in the closet or behind the shower curtain.

"Phew." She released a breath. "There's no one here."

"Everything looks all right." Hank lowered the bat. "Anything missing?"

Maggie checked her jewelry box. She didn't have much and nothing very expensive. Everything else of value was still in place. Her TV sat on the TV cabinet. Her computer monitor sat on her tiny kitchen island. Thankfully, she'd had her laptop in the Jeep with her.

Wait. Her heart hit her ribs. She'd brought her old Phantom drone home with her. She'd already uploaded the images and footage off it automatically to the cloud at the office, but she liked to make a backup on a hard drive at home as well.

She rushed over to the box on the coffee table, then flipped the lid open.

Her heart sank to her toes. "No."

Her drone was gone.

"Shit," Hank muttered. "Someone took your fancy drone."

"Yes, dammit." Her fingers curled into her palms, nails biting into her skin.

"You insured?"

She nodded. She was, thank the Lord.

Hank gripped her shoulder and squeezed. "Then it'll be okay."

Swallowing, she nodded. It would take some time, but she could replace the drone. But with her Phantom gone and her new Inspire in pieces, she'd have to rent a drone until the insurance money came through. *Dammit.*

"Thanks so much, Hank."

He eyed her face. "You sure you're okay? Want me to call someone?"

Maggie dredged up her smile. "I'll be fine. I need to call the police and report the theft. You know me, I'm tough."

"Yeah. All right. But if you need anything, Anita and I are just across the hall."

"Thanks again, Hank."

She saw him out and locked the door. Suddenly, a wave of tiredness hit. For the first time in a long time, she wished she wasn't tough. Wished that she could call someone to help. Someone she could trust to be there for her, not to lecture her on her locks like her father would.

Ace's face swam into her head and she shoved it away hard.

No. Maggie knew the best path was always to depend on yourself. When you opened up, people invariably cut you and left you hurting.

Pulling out her phone, she called the police.

THE GORGEOUS PICTURE of the Golden Gate Bridge, with the morning sun and fog shrouding it, was perfect.

Sitting at her laptop and monitor on her kitchen island, Maggie was trying to get some work done. She hadn't slept that well. Every noise had woken her. She'd ended up wedging a chair under the handle of her front door for added security.

Getting robbed sucked.

The police had come, looked around and done their thing, and taken her statement. They'd also talked to Hank. They'd told her that there had been some thefts in the area, and they weren't hopeful of getting her drone back. She'd already lodged a claim with her insurer.

She saved the image of the Bridge with the ones she wanted to upload to her website. The best ones she sold exclusively, the good ones she put on the stock sites. She clicked through more of them. She had some great aerials of Angel Island, Alcatraz, the city skyline.

She still needed to go through the footage from the trip to Muir Woods. Thankfully, she hadn't lost it with the drone since it was in the cloud.

She was sure she'd gotten some good shots of the forest, the redwoods, and the beaches.

She picked up an apple and bit into it. She also needed a clone of herself, or more hours in the day to get all this done.

And a baby was going to take up a lot of time. The apple turned to powder in her mouth.

What if she couldn't do it all? What if she was a

terrible mother? What if she screwed this whole thing up?

Maggie shook her head. She couldn't let the doubts creep in.

Suddenly, she had a craving for a grilled-cheese sandwich. It was late Sunday morning, so not far away from lunchtime. She'd been queasy again this morning, so she figured she could blame the apple seed. She'd looked up online how big the baby would be, and apparently it was the size of a seed.

So tiny. She pressed a hand to her belly.

Anyway, the queasiness had passed.

Her phone vibrated with a message.

Sleep well?

Maggie smiled at the text and bit into her apple again.

Average.

Wish I could've been there.

She shivered and ignored that comment.

How did the job go?

Fine. Ran late. Actually, I'm in the office with Vander now. I'm almost finished here. Why don't you head over to my place? If you beat me there, I can let you in remotely.

Of course, he could. No doubt Ace had the fanciest security system in all of San Francisco.

Okay, but fair warning, I'm starving.

Don't worry, gatinha, *I'll feed you.*

Smiling, Maggie shut down her computer and grabbed her bag. She was wearing jeans, and she'd topped them with a pretty, white, peasant-style blouse. She paused to put on some lipstick.

Not that she was dressing up for him. *Nope.* She would talk with Ace about the baby, but that was it. No touching, no kissing, no anything else.

She was about to head out when her cell phone rang.

The word *Mom* came up on the screen, and she smiled. Her mom and dad loved their retired life down in Monterey. Katherine "Kiki" Lopez was blonde, trim, and perpetually happy. She lived to keep a lovely house, cook for her husband, and entertain when they had friends over. She loved her only daughter, even when Maggie left her slightly bewildered. Maggie and her mom had zero in common, although she knew her mom loved her.

"Hey, Mom."

"Hi, sweetie. Are you having a relaxing Sunday?"

"Sure. How are you and Dad?"

"Good. Your father's just arrived home from golf."

After selling his small aviation business, Leo Lopez had thrown his energy into improving his golf game.

"When can you come down for a visit? You should come and stay for a week."

Maggie sighed. It was a familiar story. "Mom, you know I can't leave my business for that long. I promise to try to get down for a midweek visit when I'm not so busy."

Her mom let out a gusty sigh. "You work too hard."

"I know, Mom. But soon. I...have some news to share."

Kiki gasped. "You've met someone."

Maggie rested her head against the wall. She couldn't keep the pregnancy hidden forever. After the shock, her mom would be excited. Her dad would be, too—after he said "I told you so," and ranted about unwed mothers for a while.

"No."

"So, what is it?" her mom asked.

"It wouldn't be a secret if I told you now," Maggie said in a teasing tone that sounded pained to her own ears.

Her mom laughed. She had a sweet laugh. "You're such a tease, sweetie. You want to talk to your dad?"

"Not today. I'm on my way out. Tell him hi from me." She could do without the interrogation on her business finances today.

"All right. Have a great day, Maggie. Love you."

"Love you too, Mom."

Maggie headed out to her Jeep and jumped in. She stuck the key in the ignition, turned...and nothing.

"Oh, come on." She turned the key again and the engine made a sluggish noise. She growled and thunked her head on the steering wheel. "You piece of shit."

She tried again. The engine made an ugly sound.

She whacked the steering wheel and yanked her phone out again. She dashed off a quick text to Ace.

Jeep won't start. Might be delayed.

She got out and opened the hood, then peered in. She was no expert, but nothing seemed wrong.

She climbed back in to try again, and it still wouldn't start. Where was Gus when she needed him?

Her cell phone rang. Ace's name flashed on the screen.

"Hey," she said.

"What's wrong?"

"My Jeep is a piece of crap."

"You need a new ride, *querida*."

She snorted. "Once I pay off my other ride. The one with rotors. Which will be when I'm ready to retire."

He laughed.

"We can't all drive sexy, red Porsches like some people," she said.

"Hey, leave my Porsche out of it. Why don't you get a Lyft or an Uber?"

"I'll try one more time. Maybe the gods will smile on me. You leaving for home now?"

"Soon. Vander is a workaholic."

"I heard that." Vander's faint voice in the background.

"You're only just working that out now?" Maggie said. "He needs a woman."

"I'm not sure any are brave enough to take him on." Ace laughed.

Maggie felt that laugh low in her belly. He had such a sexy laugh.

No, you aren't allowed to notice his sexy laugh.

"Okay, see if your Jeep starts," he said. "Then get your ass to my place."

"Bossy."

"I seem to recall you liking when I got bossy with you in my bed." Ace's voice dropped to a low murmur.

She had an instant, vivid memory of him pinning her arms to the bed, thrusting inside her. Her panties were damp in a second.

"*Ace.*" She fumbled the phone and it fell out the open car door. "Now I've dropped my phone." She climbed out to grab it. "If my phone's cracked, I'm going to—"

Everything exploded with a massive boom.

***

ACE'S BODY LOCKED TIGHT, his hands clenching on the phone so hard it cracked.

That was an *explosion.*

"Maggie! Maggie!" he yelled.

No response. The line had gone dead.

Vander sprinted through the doorway. "What's going on?"

Ace felt a ball of horrible dread in his gut. His mouth was bone dry.

Pull it together, Oliveira.

"I was talking to Maggie. Her Jeep wouldn't start. *Fuck.*"

"What?" Vander barked.

"There was an explosion. The call went dead." He met Vander's dark-blue gaze. "Vander, fuck."

Vander's dark-blue eyes narrowed, and his lean face took on a hard edge. "Let's go. I'll drive. She at home?"

Ace nodded, and grabbed his phone and tablet.

They raced through the Norcross Security office. Vander had bought a warehouse in South Beach and gutted it. His apartment was on the top level, and the middle level housed the open-plan, industrial-style offices with lots of steel, concrete, and wood. The bottom level was parking for the fleet of Norcross vehicles, the gym they all used, and several holding rooms.

They sprinted down the stairs. There was a row of black BMW X6 SUVs.

Vander leaped into the closest one. Ace circled the hood and jumped in the passenger seat.

Fuck. Maggie, please be okay.

He clipped his belt in, then hunched forward. Vander tore out of the parking garage and onto the street.

"That new drone of hers went crazy yesterday. It aimed straight for her. *Shit.* I knew something was off." He should've trusted his gut.

"You think someone's targeting her?" Vander glanced over, before looking back at the road.

"I don't know."

"Check the police scanner."

Ace grabbed his tablet, swiped and tapped. He pulled up the police audio feed. His gut dropped away. "Reports of an explosion in the Marina District." He slammed his fist into the dash.

"Hold it together, Ace."

"Vander... She's pregnant."

Vander cursed. "Maggie? Maggie is having a baby?"

Ace nodded.

"And who the fuck is the asshole who knocked her up?" Vander growled.

Ace swallowed. "That asshole would be me."

Vander's knuckles turned white on the wheel. "You and I are gonna have a fucking conversation, Oliveira."

"I just found out. We're...working things out."

Vander nodded. "That's why you were so edgy to get back while you were in New York and New Orleans."

Ace looked out the window. "Yeah. I didn't know she was pregnant, but she was avoiding me. I wanted to talk to her."

Staring at the blur of the city, he did something he hadn't done in a long time, and prayed.

The SUV screamed onto Maggie's street. Police cars, an ambulance, and a fire truck were already on-scene.

Ace leaped out of the vehicle before Vander even stopped, and ran down the street.

Then he saw the black mass of the Jeep. Firefighters were pouring water on it to douse the flames.

Bile filled his mouth. *No.*

He stumbled to a stop in the middle of the street and felt like he was being torn open. "Maggie, no." Emotion swelled in his chest, threatening to knock him down.

A hand clamped on his shoulder. Vander moved close beside him, his boss' gaze on the burning vehicle, his face terrible.

A man in a suit spotted them. He ducked under the police barricade and headed their way.

Detective Hunter "Hunt" Morgan. The former Delta Force soldier was tight with the Norcross crew, even when he bitched about cleaning up after them. His brown hair was cut short, and he kept his body as fit as when he'd been in the military. He had a gun strapped to his hip, and a badge clipped to his belt.

"Figured you guys would show up." Hunt's gaze sharpened on them. "Fuck, guys." He pointed.

Blindly, Ace turned his head.

And spotted Maggie sitting on the curb, a blanket wrapped around her shoulders, her face lined with soot. A paramedic was hovering over her.

Air rushed back into Ace's lungs. He blindly tossed his tablet in Vander's direction, and broke into a sprint.

Fuck. He couldn't breathe. She was alive.

"Maggie!"

Her head jerked up. Her face was so pale.

"Ace!" She leaped up.

He swept her into his arms. "Jesus." He buried his face in her hair.

She was shaking. "The car exploded, Ace. I—" Her voice cracked.

He held her tighter and breathed her in. She smelled like smoke, but under that was the vanilla scent that was all Maggie.

"Maggie," Vander said.

She looked up at Vander. "Hi."

"You all right?"

Ace reluctantly released her so Vander could give her a hug.

"Yeah," she replied, a tremble in her voice.

"You're really okay." Ace gently pressed his palm to her belly. Warmth filled her cheeks and she pressed a hand over his, then darted a quick look at Vander.

"I told him," Ace said.

"Oh. Yes, we're okay."

"She's damn lucky." A slim, male paramedic nodded at them. "She got out of the vehicle to get her dropped phone, and the explosion blew right past her."

"The blast knocked me onto the road." She shuddered.

Ace pulled her against his chest. "She's pregnant."

The paramedic nodded. "She told me. Not far along, and she didn't get a blow to the stomach, so everything should be fine. You feel unwell, or have any bleeding, you get checked out right away."

"Thank you." She burrowed against Ace.

He held her tighter, and met Vander's gaze over her head. His boss nodded and strode over to Hunt.

Ace wanted to know what the hell had happened. Two "accidents" in two days was tripping every one of his instincts.

He led Maggie back to the curb. He sat, then pulled her into his lap. He ran his hands over her arms. He couldn't stop touching her. He needed to keep reassuring himself that she was okay.

"God, I should've replaced the Jeep ages ago," she said. "It's old, but it's always been reliable."

Ace bit his tongue. He didn't want to worry her before he had more intel. Vander would find out what the hell had happened. Right now, Ace's priority was Maggie.

He tipped her face up. She had soot streaked on her cheeks and a small scrape on her jaw. Her pretty white shirt was smeared with dirt.

He let his gaze trace her face. So damn beautiful. He pressed a gentle kiss to her lips.

She let out a little sigh. "Stop."

His gut clenched. She was determined to push him away and keep a wall between them.

Her hands clenched on his shirt. "I can't do gentle right now. I want to kiss you so much."

Damn. His cock swelled. He tugged her tighter. "I'll save it for later."

Her fingers flexed on him. Then Vander appeared, his face grim.

Ace's muscles tightened.

"I spoke to Hunt," Vander said.

"And?" Ace prompted.

"It was a car bomb."

Maggie's head jerked up and she sucked in a sharp breath. "What?"

"There was a bomb in your car, Maggie," Vander said.

Ace sucked in a breath. "Someone's trying to kill you."

"That's *insane*," she breathed, fear in her voice.

He tightened his hold on her. No way he'd let anyone get to her. Whoever this fucker was, they'd have to go through him.

CHAPTER SIX

S he couldn't stop shaking.

Maggie tugged the blanket closer. She huddled in the backseat of the X6 as Vander drove. Ace sat beside her, holding her hand.

Someone had tried to kill her. Tried to *blow* her up. She hunched her shoulders. It all seemed like a really bad dream.

Ace slid an arm across her shoulders. He was so big and warm, and she leaned into him. God, he smelled good.

She wasn't used to leaning. She'd always done things her way, always out to prove herself.

When they pulled into the parking area at Norcross Security warehouse, she watched some of the tension leak out of both men. She realized suddenly just how vigilant they'd been on the drive.

"Come on." Ace helped her out and they followed Vander upstairs to the offices.

No one was there on a Sunday.

"I'll make you a coffee—" Ace hesitated. "Or a tea."

"Tea would be good."

Vander watched her with his dark eyes. They looked black at first glance, but were a deep midnight blue.

He led her to Ace's office. It was the only one apart from Vander's without glass walls. Ace needed the walls as they were covered in computer screens. This was his little high-tech lair.

Vander pulled a chair out. Maggie shed the blanket and sat. She was still a little shaky and she gripped her hands together.

"I've flown combat missions." She shook her head. "I shouldn't be this shaky."

Vander crouched in front of her. The guy had a scary edge, but Maggie had always liked it. She knew there was no one better to have in your corner.

"It's different when you don't see the threat coming," he said. "And it's not just your life at stake."

Her pulse jumped and she pressed a hand to her belly. "I guess."

"Whatever help you need, you've got it." He paused. "This thing with Ace. He didn't..."

Maggie raised a brow. "Coerce me? Talk me into something I didn't want?"

"He's older and more experienced."

"Jeez, Vander. Not by that much. I'm twenty-seven, not seventeen. You know him. He's a good guy. And I've wanted him pretty much since I first saw him."

Vander rose and held up a hand. "No details. It's bad enough watching Gia and Saxon kissing all the time."

Maggie grinned. Vander had always treated her like a sister, while still respecting her skills.

"Then I won't tell you how good Ace is between the sheets."

Vander made a choked sound.

Already feeling steadier, the banter making her feel almost normal again, Maggie looked up as Ace walked in with a steaming mug.

Mmm, he was good in the sheets. She studied his face and the sexy stubble, and desire roared to life, leaving her tingly. She licked her lips. She wasn't sure if she should blame the pregnancy hormones, or the near-death experience. Or if it was just her regular reaction to Ace Oliveira.

"Here." He handed her the mug.

"Thanks." She sipped the tea. Loaded with cream and sugar, just how she liked it.

Ace leaned back against his desk. Vander crossed his arms over his chest.

"So, we need to work out who planted the bomb in your car, and why they want you dead," Vander said.

The hot tea burned her tongue. "Seriously, I can't think of anyone. Who the hell tries to kill someone?"

"Lots of people." Vander's tone was devoid of emotion, and darkness moved in his eyes.

Maggie fought back a shiver. Looking at him, she knew he'd seen too much of the world's darkness.

"You don't have a beef with anyone?" Ace asked.

"No. I guess you, since you didn't believe this baby was yours."

Vander's head whipped around.

Ace scowled. "That's settled. I was shocked and being an idiot."

Maggie's lips quirked briefly. "I get the odd displeased customer. A flight isn't what they expected, or the weather's not what they'd hoped for. Some people leave crappy reviews for the hell of it." She shrugged. "Nothing that I could think of would cause someone to kill me."

"It has to be connected to the drone incident," Ace said.

"When Maggie's drone went crazy?" Vander asked.

"Yeah. Her new drone got hacked. They aimed it *right* at her."

Vander cursed.

Maggie straightened. "Um..."

"What?" Ace demanded.

"My apartment was broken into last night."

Both men stiffened, and rage filled Ace's face.

"When?" he barked. "Were you home?"

"No. I found the door ajar when I got home last night."

Ace leaned over and swiveled her chair to face him. "Why the hell didn't you call me?"

"They were gone, I—"

He growled. "You call me."

She lifted her chin. "You don't run my life, Oliveira."

He made another sound. "Why do you have to be so damn independent all the damn time?"

"Because I know the only person I can depend on is *myself*."

He stared at her.

Vander cleared his throat. "Was anything taken?"

She nodded. "They stole my older drone. The assholes."

"What was on it?" Ace asked.

"Nothing special. Just scenery footage I'd taken. I still have it all backed up to the cloud."

"Anything else stolen?" Vander asked.

She shook her head. "They left my TV, and all the other electronics."

"Must be connected to her work," Vander mused.

"We'll look at all your jobs for the last two weeks," Ace said. "See if everyone checks out."

Maggie gave a tired nod and pushed her hair behind her ear. "I have the records electronically on my computer. I can email them to you."

"I can get them." He leaned over to tap on a keyboard.

She rolled her eyes. "You're going to hack my system?"

He pressed a key dramatically. "Already have."

She leaned forward and saw her client database on one screen. God, he was good.

Vander laughed. "You know he was part of the NSA's infamous Red Team?"

She spun. "No. What's that?"

"Vander," Ace growled.

"They're like the special forces of the cybersecurity world. The government's best and stealthiest hackers."

She blinked. She'd known he was good, but this was something else.

"Security pros talk about Red Team with breathless admiration," Vander continued.

Ace shot him a look. "Are you done?"

"I could go on."

"So, were you really on this special team?" she asked.

"I was a member of the NSA's Vulnerability Analysis and Operations Group." His tone warned he was done. He sank into a chair, his fingers flying. "I'll set up background searches on all of them, and then check any CCTV on your street."

Vander nodded. "See if we can get an image of whoever planted the bomb."

Bomb. Fear swooshed through her. "If I hadn't dropped my phone—" Her voice cracked.

Ace whirled, and then she was in his arms.

She clutched his shirt. "I'll be okay."

"You don't have to be. I'm right here. Just hold on."

She did, slowly breathing until she was calm again.

"Okay." She blew out a breath and sat down again. "I've got a lock on it." Then she felt a trickle of anger. "I can't *believe* some asshole thought he had the right to kill me. I want to find him, and—"

"Okay, okay, settle down." Grinning, Ace turned to his screens. "Let's see what we can find."

His fingers danced. He was amazing to watch. Information whizzed up on the screens. Maggie was afraid to admit that she typed with two fingers, and her main fix for IT problems was switching her computer off and back on again.

Ace leaned back. "There are a few CCTV cameras on Maggie's street. Not all great angles."

Three screens showed her street. She identified her Jeep parked at the edge of two of them.

Vander stood behind Ace's chair. "Let's see what we've got."

Ace wound back the footage.

When she saw herself heading to her Jeep, her heart pounded. When the explosion followed, the tang of bile filled her mouth.

A muscle ticked in Ace's jaw, and she watched herself, lying flat on the ground.

He went back to earlier in the day. Cars were coming and going, people walking dogs, kids skipping along the sidewalk.

They went through into the night.

"There," Vander said.

Maggie didn't see anything.

The timestamp said 1:06 AM. The dead of night. She peered at the screen and then noticed a dark shadow.

"Big guy," Vander said.

Ace stared at the screen, his mouth a flat line.

The man disappeared, and with a jolt, Maggie realized he was under her Jeep.

He reappeared and strolled off down the street. Relaxed. Like he wasn't a damn murderer.

Ace tapped. He caught the guy on another camera and then growled. "No clear view of the fucker's face."

"Run facial recognition anyway," Vander said. "See if anything pops."

Ace swiveled in his chair and his dark eyes met hers. "You're moving in with me."

Maggie blinked. "What?"

"You heard me."

"Ace—"

He yanked her out of her chair and gripped her jaw.

"Someone is trying to kill you. I'm *not* gonna let that happen. Until we catch him, you're staying with me."

―――――

ACE LET Maggie through the front door of his place ahead of him.

As he carried her bag in, he paused to scan the street behind them. No one appeared to be watching them.

They'd stopped by her apartment and she'd packed her things. The burnt-out hull of her Jeep had been taken away by the police. She was a little subdued, and he hated seeing her usual feisty liveliness dimmed.

The fucker who'd tried to hurt her would pay.

"I have a top-of-the-line security system," he told her.

"Of course, you do." She smiled, although it was missing its usual wattage. "Ace Oliveira, tech genius, wouldn't have any crappy system."

He pinched her butt lightly. "You'll be safe here."

"I know."

He didn't tell her that he'd been fielding calls from Gia, Harlow, Haven, and Sofie. They'd all wanted to check to see if she was okay. He'd warned them off descending, en masse. Maggie needed some peace and calm.

They stopped at the base of the stairs, staring at each other. Damn, he really wanted to kiss her.

Ace was acutely conscious of the fact that she'd had a big shock, and she was depending on him for her safety.

"Let's get you settled." He dragged his gaze off her mouth and headed upstairs.

He showed her into a guest room down the hall from his master.

"Bathroom's through there." He jerked his head.

"It's great, Ace."

"You hungry?"

"I am. I guess almost getting blown up stimulates the appetite."

His gut roiled. He strode to her and cupped her cheek. "*Querida*, let's not make jokes about that."

"Ace—"

"No." He fought back the horror trying to seep in, of how he'd felt only a few hours ago. "Today, driving to your place, I thought you were fucking dead, Maggie. When I saw your Jeep..." *Fuck*. He sucked in a breath.

Her gaze roamed his face, her gaze softening. "Okay, Ace. No jokes."

He nodded and stepped back. "Let's see what I've got to eat."

In the kitchen, he set her up on a stool at his island, and opened his fridge.

He cooked occasionally—like the dinner he'd made her—but the rest of the time, his parents dropped off food, or he ordered takeout. Aline Oliveira was perpetually worried that her oldest son didn't eat enough, and regularly dropped off things that Ace's dad made.

He pulled out a tray of little pies with a flaky pastry, and popped some in the microwave.

"What's that?" Maggie asked.

"Brazilian empadas. Not to be confused with Spanish empanadas."

"I like empanadas."

"Then you'll love these. Empadas are round, not crescent shaped. These ones are filled with chicken, olives, and requeijão. A Brazilian cream cheese."

Her eyes went wide. "Sounds great. Did you make them?"

He smiled. "No. My cooking skills don't extend that far. My father made these."

"They live close? Your folks?"

"In Bernal Heights." He pulled plates out and set one in front of her. "And my brother, Rodrigo, is in a care facility not far from here."

"He has a disability?"

"A brain injury from a drug overdose in his teens. He's a great guy. We game together, and he's addicted to making models. Usually cars and planes." He paused. "Your parents are south of here, right?"

She nodded. "Monterey. My mom cooks and gardens, and walks on the beach. Dad golfs."

Ace ate a forkful of his pie standing up. "You're close?"

She shrugged. "Fairly close. I'm an only child, and let's just say, my mom and dad are both a bit perplexed not to have a child exactly like them. My mom is the stereotype of the blonde, American housewife. She loves me, but often gives me this look like she can't quite understand where I came from. Becoming a helicopter pilot, joining the Navy, it all left her perplexed." Maggie sighed. "My father is third-generation American. His family are originally from Guatemala. He's a self-made man, owned a small fleet of planes. He sold them for several million dollars before he retired. He believes a man provides...and that I shouldn't be in debt, running a business, or having a career."

Ace heard the frustration and bitterness in her voice.

"How can they not be proud of everything you've done? You served your country. You've used your grit and skill to start a kickass business." His anger flared. "Fuck them. If they don't understand, they're crazy."

She smiled. "Thanks."

Shit. He wanted to touch her. Desperately. He focused on his food.

"This is *so* good," she said.

"Dad's a great cook."

Maggie licked her lips and damned if Ace didn't feel it in his cock.

She cleared her throat. "So, I have some jobs tomorrow—"

Ace frowned. "You can't go to work. It isn't safe."

Her head snapped up. "Ace, I have to work."

"And let this fucker have easy access to you? No."

Her fork clattered to her plate and she jumped off the stool. "Ace, if I don't work, I can't pay my loans, and I lose Hetty. I lose everything. With a baby on the way, I can't afford that."

"I'll take care of you," he growled.

That stubborn chin he knew all too well jutted out. "I can take care of myself. I'm not letting whoever this asshole is tank my business. And if you want to help support our child, that's great, but I won't be dependent on you."

Their child.

The word stole his breath. With everything that had happened, he hadn't had time to really think about the fact that Maggie was pregnant.

With a baby.

Their baby.

He blew out a breath. "I'm going to take care of you whether you like it or not."

She leaned across the island. "Ace, I need to work."

He rubbed the back of his neck. "I know."

She blinked. "Oh."

"You were ready for a fight, *gatinha*?"

"I was. A big one."

"I'll talk to Vander and we'll set up a bodyguard schedule. If I can't be with you, I'll make sure someone else is."

She frowned. "I know how much Vander charges, and you guys are busy."

"Fuck the cost. I don't care, and neither does Vander. That's the deal. Take it or leave it."

She ran a hand through her hair. "Fine."

"Good." He rose and took the plates to the sink. "Now, you still hungry?"

She cocked her head. "Have you got anything sweet?"

Ah, he'd forgotten his *gatinha* had a sweet tooth. "I might have some chocolate."

Her eyes sparked. "Gimme."

Shaking his head and grinning, he got the block of chocolate. She tore into it and moaned.

Shit. He had it bad when watching a woman eat chocolate turned him on.

"Up for a game of Skydrift Infinity?"

She froze with a square of chocolate halfway to her lips. It was her favorite flying game. "You have a fancy screen and gaming system somewhere?"

"Yep."

A smile curled her lips. "Then bring it on, Oliveira. Be prepared to get outflown."

CHAPTER SEVEN

"No, no, no." Maggie leaned forward, jerking on the Xbox controller.

She and Ace were in the middle of an epic battle of Skydrift Infinity, their colorful planes barreling through the fast-paced race.

He was sprawled beside her on the big couch, a half smile on his lips. His movie room kicked ass. The screen was huge, and a comfy, U-shaped couch sat in front of it.

"Got to move faster than that, *gatinha*."

"I'll show you faster."

Her plane darted across some lava and she fired her weapons. He dodged, his low chuckle sending shivers through her.

She was totally blaming pregnancy hormones. It felt like everything he said, every shift of his body, she noticed. And felt it low in her belly.

She couldn't afford to fall for him. The risk was far too great.

She licked her lips and focused on the screen.

Life had dumped scary on top of complicated. She was pregnant, and hadn't had a chance to truly process that yet, and now someone was trying to kill her.

Dios.

"Maggie?"

She looked up and realized that she'd lost focus, and her plane exploded in a fireball. "Sorry."

He paused the game and set his controller down on the coffee table. "What's going on in that head of yours?"

She pulled in a shaky breath. "Everything. I mean, I've had no time to process the fact that I'm going to have a baby."

His gaze dropped for a second to her belly. "It's a lot to take in."

"And now someone is trying to kill me." She shook her head. "I understood the risk I was taking when I was in the Navy. My helo was shot at, but this—" she flung an arm out "—being attacked on my own street, for no apparent reason..."

Ace grabbed her hand and squeezed. "We're going to work it out."

She had a sudden thought. He was going to guard her, be her shield. What if he got hurt? Her stomach tried to turn itself inside out at the thought.

"Ace..."

"Shh." He slid close and pulled her against him.

She fit perfectly against his body, her head on his shoulder. Her gaze fell on the sexy tattoos on his arm, and her eyes traced over the ink.

"Tomorrow, we'll go through anyone on your client list who doesn't check out. My program's crawling through the data. We'll look into anyone with debts, with secrets."

"It just doesn't make any damn sense."

He kissed the top of her head.

Heat curled through her and she slid a hand onto his thigh. What if, just for a little while, she could escape all this madness? Yes, she had to guard her heart, but that didn't mean she had to deny herself completely, right? Just for one night, she could feel safe and wanted.

She felt his muscles flex.

"Maggie..."

She turned her head and pressed her lips to the side of his neck.

His hands tightened on her. "We aren't doing this."

She stilled. He'd kissed her yesterday. Was he suddenly turned off now, knowing she was pregnant?

She looked down, to see the bulge in his jeans. Her lips curled. No, that wasn't it. She walked her fingers closer, but he caught them. God, she loved his hands.

"You've had a rough day, *gatinha*."

God, he was being nice, noble. Those weren't words she'd thought she'd ever use to describe Ace Oliveira.

"Yes, and coping just fine, thanks to you." She nipped his neck. "You came for me when I needed you. You're protecting me."

He groaned and she ran her teeth and tongue down his salty skin, causing his groan to deepen.

"You don't owe me anything for that."

"I know." She cupped his cock through the denim. "I haven't stopped thinking about that night."

With a harsh sound, he moved.

She found herself flat on her back on the couch, pinned under his hard body.

"Ace," she breathed.

"I'm trying to do the right thing. You need rest."

"I know what I need." She gripped the side of his head and kissed him.

He paused for a second, then his tongue plunged into her mouth. She pressed up into him and purred.

She bit his lip. He had the sexiest lips. "What I need is to forget for a little while."

He groaned. "You're a troublemaker."

She realized that she desperately wanted to be his troublemaker. Her heart did a crazy little dance. *No.* Sex only. This would end eventually, and Ace would head back to his carefree-bachelor life. She had to keep a tight lock on her feelings.

Life had taught her that it was better to protect yourself. People could bruise you so easily, like her dad often did, without even meaning to.

Stop thinking, Maggie.

That's what she wanted. Just for a little while.

She pulled Ace's head back to hers. The kiss was hard, their tongues tangling. She rubbed against him, and that hard cock pressed right where she wanted it.

Ace tore his mouth free. "I'm not fucking you."

She frowned, desire leaving her edgy and restless. "Why not?"

"Because I'm being a good guy here. I'm putting you first."

She pouted. "By leaving me all hot and bothered and horny?"

He shot her a sexy grin. His hair had slipped from its tie, framing his lean face. "You horny, *gatinha*?" He stroked a hand down her side.

She arched up. "Yes."

"Then maybe I can do something about that."

Both his hands stroked down and unbuttoned her jeans.

Mmm, she loved those clever hands of his. Ace had long, talented fingers.

He shifted, pulling her jeans and panties off. Maggie was soaked, her breath already coming in little pants.

"Look at you," he murmured, stroking her thighs. "All long and sexy."

She wrinkled her nose. "You mean straight up and down."

He cupped her hip. "You have curves where it counts."

The look in his eyes left no doubt that he liked what he saw. He pushed her shirt up, hesitated, then he pressed soft kisses to her flat belly.

Oh. The hit of emotion shocked her. He was kissing right over where their child was growing.

He moved lower, pushing her thighs apart. "The sounds you made when I fucked you have haunted my dreams." He stroked his fingers up her thighs.

"*Ace*." Her hips jerked up.

"When I was away, I jerked off, thinking about you. You taking my cock, stroking my cock, sucking my cock."

Maggie moaned. "So let me have it."

"Not yet. First, I'm going to spend some time with this pretty pussy."

He lowered his head.

Oh. *God.*

He licked her, and her head shot back into the cushions. He held her thighs apart and took his time driving her crazy. Every lick was designed to stimulate.

He bit her inner thigh. "You like me licking you, *gatinha*?"

"*Yes.*"

"You taste like fucking heaven."

His tongue stabbed into her and she gripped his hair and moaned.

"How about when I suck you?"

She panted. "Sucking is good, too."

"Hmm, let's see." His tongue swirled around her clit. Her cries turned garbled, and then he sucked.

"Ace." She bucked and jerked.

"Maybe you need my fingers, too?" He thrust two inside her.

Her cries turned frantic now, pleasure growing so huge that it was hard to breathe. He kept thrusting, his mouth back on her clit. The pleasure arrowed through her, and then her world exploded.

She screamed his name, tugging on his hair.

When Maggie opened her eyes, she felt too damn lazy to move. Little aftershocks of pleasure were still rippling through her.

Ace leaned over her, a smug masculine look on his face. His lips glistened.

"It's not conclusive if you preferred the licking or sucking. I might need to conduct a few more tests."

She laughed. God, when had she laughed during sex

with a guy? For her, it had always been about a quick, fun tussle, then she'd be on her way.

A guy had never held back his own pleasure, and taken his time to see what she really liked.

"Bed for you." With that announcement Ace rose, then scooped her up off the couch.

Maggie was tall, and Ace was lean, but he carried her with ease. There was strength in that rangy body of his.

She snuggled into him as he carried her down the hall to the guest room.

"You're going to sleep now, knowing you're safe."

He sat on the bed. She looked at the bulge in his jeans. "You could stay."

"We both know we wouldn't be sleeping if I stayed." He smiled. "I'm going to jerk off in the shower, picturing you clenching on my cock."

Her womb spasmed. "Ace."

"Sleep well, *gatinha*."

———

IT WAS a scream that woke Ace.

He leaped out of his tangled sheets and grabbed his Glock off the bedside table.

In just his boxers, he sprinted out of his bedroom, his blood pumping. The alarm hadn't gone off, nor had his external sensors. No one could be inside.

He raced into Maggie's room. She sat in the middle of the bed, shaking and breathing harshly.

"Maggie?" He scanned the room. There was nobody there.

He didn't get a reply. It was like she didn't see him.

He set the gun on the bedside table and snapped on the lamp.

She was staring ahead, almost hyperventilating. Then she started slapping her arms. "I'm on fire," she cried.

Ace slid into the bed and pulled her close. "You're fine, Maggie. You're all right. You're at my place."

She pulled in a shuddering breath and blinked. "Ace?"

"I'm here, baby. Just hold on."

With a sob, she buried her face in his neck. She wound her arms around him and held on tight.

He stroked her back. She was only wearing a tiny, black tank top and panties.

Ignoring those luscious, long legs, he kept stroking her, murmuring soothing words in her ear.

After one more shudder, she relaxed. "*Dios.*"

"*Deus* in Portuguese," he said, trying to lighten the mood. "Nightmare?"

She nodded. "The bomb went off, and I was on fire."

"It's a normal reaction."

She made a sound. "I'm fine. I don't need to fall apart over it. I made it."

"Give yourself a break, *gatinha.*" He looked into her face. She had the crease of the pillow on one cheek, and her hair was a little mussed. She looked as cute as hell. And if he told her that, she'd probably bite him.

She shook her head. "I was never allowed to fall apart, or cry. Dad said he was raising a tough daughter."

Ace frowned. He was liking Leo Lopez even less. "You want to cry or scream, go right ahead."

Her face softened. "It's not his fault. It's how he was raised. His father was strict, and demanded a lot from his kids. And my dad wanted a son to carry on the family name. Mom had a difficult pregnancy, so the doctors recommended no more after me. I was all he got."

And the asshole should cherish the tough, gorgeous, determined daughter that he'd raised.

Ace stroked her arm. "You going to sleep now?"

There was a flash of fear in her eyes. He watched as she locked it down.

"I can stay with you until you fall asleep," he said.

She dipped her head, almost shyly. "You don't mind?"

"I don't mind."

He turned off the lamp and pulled her down beside him on the bed. They rested their heads on the pillow and he pulled her against him.

She snuggled into him and Ace tried to stay relaxed. She felt so damn good. She rested her hand on his bare chest, her sleek legs pressed against his.

His cock was hard in an instant. He swallowed a groan. At least the darkness hid it. He'd jerked off earlier, the sweet taste of her on his lips. *Shit*. He was going to need another cold shower.

"I feel safe with you."

Her quiet words were slurred with sleep. He pressed a kiss to her temple, realizing what a gift those words were. He already knew she tried to do everything herself and didn't let herself trust very easily. "I'm right here, *gatinha*. Sleep now."

He heard her breathing even out. He gently pressed a

palm to her flat belly.

Panic, awe, and a bunch of other emotions hit him. There was a baby in there. A bit of Maggie and a bit of him. Hell, it would be a terror.

Smiling, he drifted off to sleep.

WHEN ACE WOKE, sunlight was peeking around the blinds.

Maggie was half lying on top of him. Her tank top had ridden up, and her bare belly and breast were pressed against him.

His cock was so hard it hurt.

He blew out a breath. He wouldn't hurt her any more than he already had. It was his job to keep her safe.

He'd fucked it up with Rodrigo. Ace's gut churned. He wasn't going to let that happen with Maggie. He wasn't going to take his eyes off the job.

He slipped out from under her. She mumbled, but didn't wake. There were dark circles under her eyes. She was already tired, and the nightmare hadn't helped.

He watched her curl up in the bed and dragged in a breath. The punch of protectiveness almost made him stagger.

Quickly, he headed to his bedroom. He needed to shower, jerk off again, then work out how to keep her safe today.

He stripped and stepped under the water. He took his throbbing cock in hand.

As he stroked, he pressed the other palm to the tiles

and groaned. He thought of Maggie. Sweet and spicy Maggie.

He stroked harder, rougher. His groan echoed off the tiles. "Fuck, yeah, Maggie."

Something made him look up.

Maggie was standing on the other side of the glass. She was only in that tank top and those tiny panties.

Fuck.

Her gaze was glued to where he was stroking his cock, her lips parted.

"Maggie," he growled.

Her gaze jerked up. "You have such a gorgeous cock." She licked her lips. "I want to watch you blow for me."

Now Ace's growl was long and tortured. He tugged harder and she pressed one palm to the glass.

"Hand in your panties," he ordered. "I bet that little clit is swollen and needs rubbing."

She moaned, her hand sliding down her belly and into the cotton.

Just watching her made his cock swell impossibly more.

"You did this." He turned so she had a perfect view of his hard cock as he worked it. "It's your fault I'm so hard."

Her cheeks flushed; her fingers were busy. "*Ace.*"

"Watch, *gatinha.*" He felt the pleasure building, like a storm. "Watch."

"Do it."

Ace gave one last tug, then he was coming. He groaned her name as his come spurted over his hand and fell on the tiles.

A second later, she made a sound that he knew well,

her body shaking as she came.

She slumped against the glass.

"Wow," she breathed. "Hell of a way to start the day."

He smiled at her and rinsed off.

"I'd love to join you," she murmured. "But I really need to get to work."

Ace nodded. "I'm going to message Vander. I'm coming with you, and I'll work from your office."

She bit her lip. "That's going to mess with your work—"

"I don't care. And Vander won't, either. He's committed to keeping you safe. If I can't be with you, Vander or one of the other guys will."

"Thanks, Ace."

She didn't need to thank him.

Suddenly, her face went sheet-white.

"Maggie?"

She spun and ran to the toilet.

"Maggie!" He leaped out of the shower, grabbed a towel, and wrapped it around his hips.

She was crouched by the toilet, her face pale, her hand on her belly. She wasn't being sick, but he could see she was fighting it.

"Hey." He knelt beside her and rubbed her back.

"This is your fault," she said miserably.

"Totally." He'd take the blame, if it made her feel better.

She pulled in a breath. "Okay, I think it's passing. I'm not going to be sick."

Good. He hated seeing her feel unwell. "Come on, I'll make you some toast, or get you crackers, or something."

CHAPTER EIGHT

"Gus, I think I'll need to order those new bearings." Maggie wiped her hands on a rag.

The man nodded. "Yep."

Shit. Another expense. "I'll send an email. You'll put this back together?"

"On it."

She headed to the office and pushed through the door. She paused. Ace had taken over her desk. He was working on a sleek laptop and absorbed in whatever he was doing. Today, he wore a blue-checked shirt, with the sleeves rolled up. His hair was tied back in a stubby tail and he had scruff on his cheeks. Her belly pulsed. She took a second to take in the tattoo on his forearm. She remembered, vividly, tracing it with her tongue.

Then she remembered him in the shower this morning, gloriously naked and wet, jerking that long cock for her.

God, she was about to self-combust.

He looked up. "Hey, you okay?"

She nodded. "I want to put my drone up for a bit. My old one, obviously." She wrinkled her nose. "My old, old one."

He rose. "I want to check it out first. I can add some extra security to keep anyone from accessing it."

She nodded. She went to the shelf where she stored the drones and reached for the large box.

Ace shouldered in front of her. "Don't even think about carrying that."

"I think that—"

He held up his hand. "I've got it."

"Fine."

He carried the drone box outside for her. It was sunny today. Spring was well and truly trying to break through. Gus gave Ace an evil stare. Her employee hadn't been impressed when she'd turned up with Ace.

Ace crouched, and synced his tablet to the drone controller. "This'll just take a couple of minutes."

She nodded.

"Maggie?" Gus called out. "Need you to check these rotors."

"I'll be back," she told Ace.

She watched him scan the area and the fence line. She followed suit. There was no one watching today. All she could see was Ace's hot, little Porsche 911 parked by the gate. He'd driven her to work in it.

Gus stepped off a stepladder. "There's a bit of abrasion. Doesn't look too bad."

Maggie climbed up the ladder. "I've already spent a fortune on these rotors."

A second later, hard arms wrapped around her and yanked her off the ladder.

She only had time to squeak in surprise. Ace set her on the ground, his face like a thundercloud.

"Ace—"

"No ladders. No climbing. No lifting heavy things."

Okay, he was just worried, even if he was being overbearing about it. "I know my limits."

"No arguments, either."

Gus glared at Ace. "Girl has her own brain."

Maggie tried for some patience. "Look—"

"She's also pregnant," Ace said. "No climbing. No lifting."

Gus blinked, his bushy brows drawing together. "Pregnant?" His weathered face turned red. "You let some asshole knock you up?"

Maggie looked up at the blue sky for a beat. "Gus—"

"Who?" he demanded. "Where is he? Is he treating you right? If he isn't, I'll—"

"That asshole would be me." Ace crossed his arms over his chest.

The men stared at each other. Maggie smoothed a hand over her hair, waiting for a tumbleweed to roll past.

"No climbing or lifting," Ace repeated.

Gus grunted, then nodded. "Got it."

Maggie tapped her foot. "I'll just stand over here and look helpless."

Ace grinned at her, but then he looked back at Gus, his face turning serious. "And you need to keep an eye out. Someone tried to kill her yesterday."

She gasped. She hadn't told Gus. Hadn't wanted him to worry.

"Kill her?" Gus' face darkened. "What the hell are you talking about, Oliveira?"

"Someone planted a bomb in her vehicle."

Gus' brows went up. "That's why you aren't in your Jeep and you have a guard dog." Gus scowled at her. "Why didn't you tell me?"

She swallowed. "Well—"

"Because you always have to do everything yourself. Because that father of yours always makes you feel like dirt."

Her heart thumped. "Gus—"

"Always trying to prove you can do anything."

Ace was scowling too, and nodding.

Uh-oh. If these two bonded over this, she'd never hear the end of it. "I didn't want you to worry."

"Well, I'm worried." Gus looked at Ace. "Who?"

"Don't know yet. We're working on it. I'm going to install a camera in the hangar, but I need you to check the helo every day for any tampering."

A muscle ticked in Gus' jaw as he nodded. "You'd better take good care of her, Oliveira."

"That's the plan."

Maggie threw her hands up. "Hello, still over here and in charge of my life." She scowled at Ace.

For some reason, that made him grin and yank her in for a quick kiss. After leaving her breathless, he spun and strode back to the drone.

"I'll take care of the rotors." Gus turned back to Hetty. "No climbing or lifting, girlie."

She rolled her eyes. Heaven help her when she actually looked pregnant. They might just wrap her in bubble wrap.

Ace finally gave her the okay to take the drone up. She was excruciatingly conscious of him staying outside, working on his tablet, and leaning against the wall of the office building.

Keeping her safe.

Her fingers fumbled on the controller. *Dios*. She was going to fall totally in love with him. She knew it. Her pulse jittered.

She wasn't sure Ace was ready for that. What happened when she was safe, and he wanted his bachelor lifestyle back?

Maggie would end up with a broken, shattered, irreparable heart, that's what would happen.

She landed the drone and squashed all her thoughts. Right now, she had work to do, and a flight in Hetty to prepare for after lunch.

She headed back into the office, where Ace was now working.

"How did it go?" Ace asked.

"Well, my drone didn't try to kill me."

He shot her a look.

"I got some good shots. People can't get enough of good-quality pictures and footage of San Francisco, the Bridge, and the Bay."

"That's good. I ordered lunch from MaMo."

She stifled a moan. "I *love* everything from MaMo."

His brown eyes met hers, and his lips twitched. "I know. You mention it constantly. I got you arepas."

Her favorite. She was addicted to the fried corn pockets stuffed with chicken and gouda. The little restaurant specialized in food with a South American flair. A funny feeling flashed under her breastbone. He knew her so well.

As they ate lunch, Ace took a call, and Maggie savored her arepas. Her nausea from the morning was now a distant memory. She did a quick search and pulled a face. Apparently, morning sickness could occur at any time of the day, and last longer than the first trimester.

Great. She needed to tell her parents. Her mouth went dry. No rush for that one.

Ace wandered back to the office and she listened appreciatively to his low, sexy voice. The image of a baby resting on his chest as he spoke to it popped into her head from nowhere. Warmth bloomed in her chest. Would he be hands on? Talking about the baby still made him uneasy.

Suddenly, the door swung open. She expected to see Gus' grumpy face, but instead, the handsome, clean-cut face of Chris Hammett appeared. He was the guy she'd gone on a few dates with last month.

"Maggie." Chris' face twisted with concern. He was dressed in a suit, since he worked at an investment firm.

She rose. "Chris..."

She was engulfed in a hug.

"Jeez, gorgeous. I just heard about the car bomb. I was so worried. Why didn't you call?"

She blinked. She'd called him the day after her night with Ace to cancel their upcoming date and cool things off. He hadn't been happy about it, but after a few more calls, she hadn't heard from him.

"I..." She didn't know what to say. She hadn't actually given him any thought.

"Back off," a deep voice growled.

The whip of Ace's tone, now lethal, made her jolt.

Chris was yanked away, and she found herself clamped to Ace's side.

Chris' hazel eyes narrowed. "Who the fuck are you?"

"Chris—" Maggie needed to de-escalate the situation. "This is Ace. He works at Norcross Security."

"Where you work sometimes." Chris relaxed. "Is he your bodyguard?"

"He's keeping an eye on things."

"So, you're in danger?"

"Well, it's complicated." She didn't want to go into details with him. "Ace, this is Chris Hammett."

"Her boyfriend," Chris said.

Maggie's eyes went wide. *What the—?*

She felt Ace's body lock. She pressed a hand to his chest. "Chris, we went on a few dates."

"Good dates. I didn't want to cool things off. I still don't. You're smart, funny, a good kisser."

Oh. *God.* Ace's muscles flexed under her fingers.

"I'm sorry, Chris." She kept her tone gentle. "Things have changed."

"It looks like someone might be trying to hurt you. I want to help. Move in with me."

She blinked.

"She's already living with me," Ace growled.

"You're a work colleague. You can stand down."

Ace made a sound that raised the hairs on the back of her neck. She stepped in front of him and he pressed up against her back.

"Chris, it's sweet and really nice, but not what I want. I'm fine."

"Maggie, gorgeous." He held out his hands. "We were good. We've got a chance for something great."

Oh, God. "No, we don't," she said, as gently as possible.

Chris held out a hand. "Give me a—"

Ace stepped between them. "Maggie's mine."

Those words, said with so much conviction, made her jolt.

Chris' face hardened. "Look—"

"Mine," Ace repeated. "It was me watching her come this morning."

Oh, hell. She fought back a wince.

Chris stiffened.

"It's me she's living with. Me keeping her safe." Ace leaned closer. "And it's me who's the father of the baby in her belly."

Ah, Ace Oliveira. Subtle as a sledgehammer.

But then every muscle in her went tight. For the first time, he'd very much staked a claim on the child they'd made. Said he was a father. She looked at him and his gaze met hers. Something strong passed between them.

Chris recoiled, his gaze dropping to her stomach. "You're pregnant?"

"Yes," she said.

"You were fucking me and him at the same time?"

She bristled and shoved forward. "I never fucked you. We had a few dates, Chris, that's all."

"Knew you were holding back. Guess you were hedging your bets."

"No, I was getting to know you, although I already knew I didn't feel a spark."

"So, you fucked him, instead."

"Enough." Ace shoved Chris toward the door. "You're done, *amigo*."

"I'm gone." Chris stormed out.

Maggie pinched the bridge of her nose.

"Okay, *gatinha*?"

"No. Why don't you just brand your name on my forehead?"

He grinned. "Property of Ace Oliveira. Might look cute on your sexy ass."

She bristled, ready to blast him.

But he kissed her.

And her brain short-circuited.

Damn him. He was so good at it, and all the anger leaked out of her and she kissed him back.

SITTING in his office at home, Ace rolled his chair back to peek through the doorway. Maggie was in the living room, music blaring. She was dancing like a crazy woman.

He grinned. She had some moves. He watched her

swing her hips, and remembered them dancing together at the gala.

His phone rang, and he saw it was Vander.

"Hey," Ace answered.

"How is she?"

"Hanging in there."

"You find anything in your searches?"

"I have a shortlist. I'm running through all her customers." Ace shook his head. "Broad list. Honeymooners, tourists, birthdays, corporate bigwigs, businesses, scientists. It's taking longer than I thought." There was a ping from his computer. "Wait a second."

"What have you got?"

It was an image of a man. He stood in profile, but Ace could make out some of his features.

Ace smiled. "I got an image off CCTV a few blocks from Maggie's apartment. I've been searching for our bomber's clothes."

"You got a hit," Vander said.

"Yep, I'm good. Not his full face, he's in profile, but it's a start."

"Send me a copy. Don't stop digging."

Ace didn't intend to. "I won't stop until she's safe."

In the living room, Maggie started singing. She'd never sign any record deals, but she sounded happy. He grinned.

"I won't ask again how she is, since I can hear her singing," Vander said, a hint of amusement in his voice. "Take care of her, Ace."

"I am, *amigo*."

"Good."

Ace ended the call, just as his computer pinged again. "Hmm." Her last helicopter customer before the explosion was Biowave Science. It didn't exist. There was a single page on a website with a logo, but it was a non-existent company.

Ace printed a picture of the bomber. He needed to see if Maggie recognized the guy. He took a deep breath. He wasn't keen to trigger another nightmare.

He stared at the photo. This was the man who'd tried to kill Maggie. Ace ground his teeth together. He wasn't going to fail her.

He headed into the living room. She was facing away from him, swinging those slim hips.

He turned off the music.

She spun and smiled. "Sorry. Too loud?"

He shook his head and dropped onto the couch. "We need to talk."

She swallowed and sat.

"I got a picture of the bomber."

She straightened. "The police found him?"

Ace shook his head. "No. Hunt told me that the guy didn't leave any traces, and the bomb parts were all generic." Ace held out the photo. "But I found this."

She looked at the photo. "You can't see much of him. I don't recognize him."

"You sure?"

She nodded. "I'm sure."

"Vander's going to take a look and ask around. He'll touch base with all his contacts."

She rubbed her cheek and nodded again.

He cupped her face. "No one is getting to you."

Her gaze traced over his face. "Okay."

"Right, next item. Any clients tweak you? Acted strange?"

She cocked her head. "Not any that rings a bell. Some aren't nice, a bit abrupt, but nothing that shouted 'I want to kill you.'"

"A couple of customers have hit my radar. Alexis Lowe. She doesn't exist."

Maggie grinned. "That was an engaged couple. She got her fiancé a sunset joy flight, champagne included." Maggie sighed. "They were so in love. Her name is Alexis Carol. She'll be Lowe once they get married. She thought it was cute to book in his name."

Okay, scratch the romantic bride-to-be. "Biowave Science."

"The scientists?" Her eyebrows rose. "I took them out to the Muir Woods National Monument. They wanted to study the redwoods."

Ace frowned. "Biowave doesn't exist."

"What?" Her brow creased. "There were three of them. I dealt with the main guy. Dr. Spiner."

"Did he pay with a credit card?"

She stilled. "No, cash. I did think it was weird at the time. And he gave me the creeps a little."

Ace straightened. "How?"

"He was rude. Cold. He stared at me. Not in a checking-me-out way, in a cold, creepy kind of way."

"Did you see what they did at the park?"

She shook her head. "I put the drone up while Dr. Spiner and his guys headed into the trees. Actually,

Spiner wasn't happy I did. He got in my face about it after, but Vander arrived and Spiner left."

A whisper flitted across Ace's instincts. "You got his first name?"

"Um, I think it was Paul."

Ace grabbed his tablet did a quick search.

"Dr. Paul Spiner, Head of Biology at the University of San Francisco."

Maggie nodded. "That's him."

Ace swiveled the tablet. It showed a picture of an older professor, with snow-white hair.

Maggie blinked. "That's not Dr. Spiner. He was late thirties. Early forties, tops. Brown hair and blue eyes."

Yeah, Ace's instincts were pinging. "There were two guys with him?"

"One muscular guy who was shorter, with brown hair." She frowned. "The other guy was tall, with sandy-blond hair."

"And?" Ace prompted. "I see you thinking of something."

"I...just figured I hadn't been paying attention. The blond, he seemed a bit out of shape. Had a dad bod."

Ace paused. Shit, he was going to be a dad, would he get a dad bod?

"Ace?"

"Sorry, go on."

"When we returned, the blond guy looked fitter, more toned."

Ace cocked his head. "It was a different guy?"

"It can't have been. He had the same color hair, was

the same height. I just must've—" She gasped and swayed like she'd been hit.

"Maggie?" He grabbed her arm.

"Oh, God." She pressed her hand to her mouth. "That news report of a dead body in Muir Woods. On the TV. He looked like that blond guy."

Ace wasn't sure how this all fit together, but he felt like they were onto something, and it stank to high heaven.

Pulling his tablet over, he typed in a quick search.

"Dead body was found in Muir Woods. Caucasian male. Blond-brown hair. Six feet two inches. Hadn't been dead long before hikers found him. His name was Adrian Marks. He was a building inspector for the city."

"Not a scientist." She rubbed the back of her neck. "What the hell is going on? This is all just a confusing mess, and I still have no idea why someone would want to kill me."

"Someone hacked your drone and stole your other one," he said slowly.

She gasped. "You think I caught something on video that someone didn't want anyone to see?"

"Maybe. And after they stole your drone, they must have realized you'd already downloaded a copy of the data."

Her cheeks paled. "Then they tried to kill me."

"You need to check your footage."

"God." She shivered.

Ace pulled her against him and she buried her face in his neck.

Damn, he liked her right there. Warm, trusting.

He froze. Rodrigo trusted him, too.

Ace stared at his fingers in her hair. "I'm going to sort this out, *gatinha*." He pressed a quick kiss to the top of her head. "Just hold on."

Her arms snaked around him. "Okay, Ace."

So much trust. He hoped to hell he deserved it.

CHAPTER NINE

Maggie blew out a breath and tried to focus on the footage on the screen.

Ace's home office setup was a thousand times better than her old laptop perched on the tiny island in her apartment. She was using two big screens to study the last week's footage. She'd already saved a bunch of still shots and video clips.

It was hard to focus, though. She kept thinking of someone trying to kill her. The dead man in Muir Woods. Ace's kisses.

She blew out a breath and sat back. Her chair creaked. She'd woken this morning wrapped around Ace. He'd slept in her bed again.

I want to make sure those nightmares stay away. He'd whispered that to her, as she'd fallen asleep.

She closed her eyes. He was so protective. But when this crazy situation was over, what then? She had no doubt he'd support the baby financially, but at the thought of the baby, she saw the whites of his eyes.

Why? He was tight with his family. She'd met his parents a few times, and knew he was close with his brother.

He also talked about his extended family—aunts, uncles, cousins. Some were here in the US, and others back in Brazil. He'd been down to Brazil a few times to visit them.

Her stomach rumbled. Thankfully, this morning's queasiness had passed quickly. Now she was hungry. She looked at her watch. It was almost lunchtime.

She wandered into the kitchen. Ace was at work. He'd been called in for a job. She hadn't had a flight scheduled this morning, so he'd locked her up in his house with his high-tech security system on.

Maggie munched on some cheese and crackers, and got back to work. She hadn't been at it long, studying footage of the Muir Woods National Monument, when she spotted a group of men in the picture.

Frowning, she zoomed in.

There were four men.

She recognized Dr. Spiner instantly. It was the scientists.

But there were four of them? She'd only flown the three in.

It was an aerial shot, so it was hard to tell what they were doing, exactly. It didn't look like they were studying redwoods. And who was the fourth guy? A hiker, maybe?

Then she saw Spiner lift his arm. One of the men fell flat on his back and Maggie froze.

Her heart jumped into her throat. She rewound and

watched it again. There was no sound, but she was pretty sure Spiner had shot the man.

God. *God.*

She watched, heart thumping, as the other two men dragged the body into the trees.

Then the three men walked off together.

Maggie pulled in a shaky breath. She was pretty sure she'd just witnessed a murder.

Pulse racing, she ran her hands through her hair. *Dios.* She took some breaths, grabbed her phone, and called Ace.

"Hey, *gatinha*, I'm on my way home for lunch with you."

"Ace."

"What's wrong?" His tone sharpened.

"*Dios.*" She blew out a breath. "I went through the drone footage."

"And?"

"I saw the scientists. There was a fourth man in the woods. I think they killed one."

Ace hissed out a breath.

"You don't sound surprised," she said.

"I figured it was something like this. Okay, look, we'll go over it, and put the pieces together."

"Why kill me?"

"Clean up. They were afraid you'd caught the murder on the drone footage." His tone firmed. "I'm not letting them get you, *querida*. You have me, Vander, all of Norcross behind you. You're one of ours."

She pressed her fist to her chest. "Ace..."

"I know you're used to dealing with things alone, but not anymore. Lean a little, *gatinha*."

"All right, Ace."

Suddenly she heard a noise downstairs. She rose slowly.

"Maggie?"

"Hang on." She tiptoed across the living room to the top of the stairs. There was definitely someone outside.

"Ace," she whispered. "There's someone at the front door."

She heard the roar of an engine across the line. "I'm only a few minutes away, and the alarm is on."

She heard beeping. "Oh my God, they're *disarming* the alarm." She saw movement at the bottom of the stairs. "Ace, the front door's opening!"

"Get into my room, Maggie, *now*." His voice was like a whip. "Lock the door, then go into the bathroom and lock it behind you."

She ran. Nausea roared to life. No, not now. She clutched her stomach and swallowed repeatedly. She raced through his light-filled bedroom and into the bathroom.

It wasn't huge, but it was lovely. A free-standing tub sat in front of a huge window and the floor was a pretty, hexagonal marble tile.

She locked the door and backed up. Anger rose, hot and furious. She'd defend herself and her baby. She rummaged through the drawers and found a pair of scissors.

"Ace?"

"I'm nearly there, Maggie. Hold on."

"Okay."

"I'm letting you go now. Wait for me, and don't open the door to anyone else."

"Be careful, Ace."

"Always."

The next few minutes ticked by so slowly. Her cheese and crackers threatened to reappear, but she managed to avoid being sick. She stared at her pale reflection in the mirror.

Was Ace okay?

Her hands curled into her palms. What if he got hurt? *No.* She couldn't cope with that.

Uh-oh. Maggie sucked in a sharp breath. She just realized that she was hopelessly in love with him.

She hadn't guarded her heart, she'd just tumbled headlong in love.

"Maggie?" Ace's voice came through the door. "It's okay. Open up."

Relief punched through her. She raced to the door and yanked it open.

She scanned him, then threw herself into his arms. "Are you all right?"

"Fine." He stroked her back.

"God, I was so afraid. I *hate* being afraid."

He shot her that sexy grin. "I know."

She kissed him. His hands clenched on her for a second and he kissed her, then pulled back. "My parents are here."

Maggie blinked. "What?"

"They have the code. They wanted to drop some food off."

"Oh." Relief flooded Maggie. There were no murderous bad guys. *Phew*.

Wait. His parents?

"Come on." He towed her out. "They want to say hi."

"Ace... You haven't...?"

"We'll share when we're ready, Maggie. I assure you, my mom will be ecstatic."

Maggie fought the urge to fidget, and willed her churning belly to settle.

Mr. and Mrs. Oliveira sat in the kitchen. Ace looked a lot like his mom in the face, and didn't look anything like his father, who was a short, trim man with salt-and-pepper hair.

Mrs. Oliveira's face lit up. "Maggie."

"Sorry we surprised you," Mr. Oliveira said.

Maggie pinned a smile on. "I...I've got a bit of trouble, and Ace was so kind to offer me his guest room."

Best not to mention that he'd slept in there with her the last two nights.

"I raised a good boy." Mrs. Oliveira kissed Maggie's cheeks.

Her hair was still dark brown—if she was like Maggie's mom, she visited the salon religiously— and it was cut to her jaw line. Her eyes were the same coffee brown as Ace's. The woman's floral perfume hit Maggie and saliva pooled in her mouth. Her belly gave a hard kick.

Oh, no. She felt the color drain from her face.

Ace frowned. "Maggie?"

"I..." She clamped a hand over her mouth, whirled, and ran.

She reached the guest bathroom and staggered to the toilet. She was violently ill.

As she finished retching, she was conscious of Ace beside her, patting her back.

"Here." He handed her a bottle of water.

"Apparently 'morning' sickness isn't entirely accurate," she muttered.

"Feeling better?"

She nodded.

He pressed a hand to her belly and stroked gently. Warmth filled her. It seemed like that was getting easier for him.

"Leave the girl in peace, Aline." His father's voice in the hall.

"I just want to check she's okay. Maybe she has food poisoning or something?"

Ace and Maggie froze. Surely, they wouldn't come in.

"Privacy, Aline," Mr. Oliveira growled.

"Pfft, I'm being kind. She might need something."

Ace's parents appeared in the doorway.

The older couple stared at Ace and Maggie—kneeling together, Ace's hand protectively on her belly.

Mrs. Oliveira's brown eyes went wide, then they filled with happy tears. Her smile was beaming. "I had morning sickness all hours of the day when I was pregnant with Adriano and Rodrigo. It would strike out of the blue."

Ace sighed. "Mom—"

Maggie blinked at him. "Your name is Adriano?"

"No one calls me that, not even Mom."

"Let the girl up, Ace," Mrs. Oliveira said.

They rose and Mrs. Oliveira cupped Maggie's cheeks. "You're pregnant."

Maggie swallowed and nodded.

"And my boy is the father?"

Maggie glanced at Ace. She couldn't read anything in his churning gaze. She looked back at his mother and nodded again.

Then Mrs. Oliveira threw her arms around both of them. "Oh, you're going to make a *beautiful* baby."

THE NEXT MORNING, Ace woke with a slim hand lying perilously close to his hard cock.

Maggie, as he'd discovered these last few days, sprawled all over the place in bed. She was lying on her belly, fast asleep, one hand low on his gut.

He blew out a breath and thought of boring, unsexy code.

Nope, his cock was still hard.

She looked peaceful, and he didn't want to wake her. After his parents' impromptu visit yesterday, he'd taken her to the Norcross office and set her up working on her drone footage in the corner of his computer lab.

He'd gotten a copy of what she'd seen in the Muir Woods National Monument and played it for Saxon, Rhys, and Vander.

None of them had been happy about it.

"Make a copy," Vander had ordered. "I'll share it with Hunt."

Ace nodded.

"And Ace, find these assholes."

He was working on it. He'd spent most of yesterday afternoon and last night working on it. He'd find out who the fuck this Spiner guy really was, and make him regret ever daring to try and hurt Maggie.

He glanced at her again, then slipped out of bed.

He hoped he could talk her into his bed—it was bigger and comfier than his guest room one. And Maggie sure liked to sprawl.

He set some water and crackers on the bedside table, then headed to the shower to jerk off. He was dressed and eating a bagel when she came out, showered, dressed, and pale faced.

"Don't feel like breakfast?" he asked.

She shook her head. "The crackers helped though. I don't feel like puking my guts up."

"No jobs today?"

She shook her head. "I thought it best to cancel a few things."

"You're with me at the Norcross office again."

"I'll keep working on my photos." She fiddled with her hair. "Are your parents okay? About the baby?"

"Pretty sure my mom will have started a list of baby names."

"We haven't talked about how this will work. About after the baby arrives..."

"Hey." He cupped her cheeks. "We're still adjusting, and you're in danger. Let's sort that out first."

"You're afraid to be a father."

He froze. *Fuck*. "I said, give it time."

"What are you so afraid of?"

"I said, leave it." His voice was a harsh rasp.

She jerked back.

He cursed and ran a hand through his hair. "Sorry, I..." He didn't want to dredge up his worst failure. Or darker, older secrets.

"It's none of my business." Face blank, she headed back to the bedroom. "I'll grab my bag. I'll be ready to go when you are."

Ace looked at the ceiling. "Fuck."

It was a quiet drive to the Norcross office. Maggie kept busy on her phone, or staring out the window.

"Maggie—"

"It's okay, Ace. We all have our demons. You don't have to share them if you don't want to." She kept her gaze on her phone.

He reached over and gripped her thigh. "I...don't want you to look at me differently."

Her gaze flew to his face. "Will I?"

"Yeah. Probably."

"Ace, I know you. Some old secret, no matter how old, isn't going to change that."

He hoped that was the truth. He saw the Norcross warehouse ahead.

All of a sudden, a man darted across the street.

"Oh, my God," Maggie cried. "Watch out!"

Ace slammed on the brakes and narrowly missed him, but the man lunged and slammed into a parked car.

"*Merda*." Ace pulled into a parking spot on the street and turned the Porsche off.

Maggie leaped out of the car.

"Maggie, wait." He raced after her.

ANNA HACKETT

He was circling the vehicle, when Maggie reached the man.

"Are you all right?" she asked.

Suddenly, the man looked up and grabbed Maggie.

"Hey." Ace broke into a run.

The man tried to lift Maggie off her feet, but she fought. She kicked her legs and jerked her head back. The back of her skull collided with the guy's nose.

His ripe curses filled the air.

Ace lunged in and rammed his fist into the guy's side.

The man grunted and let Maggie go. Ace yanked her away.

The man straightened and pulled a knife. Maggie gasped, and Ace shoved her behind him.

The attacker slashed out.

Sloppy. Ace hadn't worked in the field as much as the other Norcross guys, but he was trained, and he worked out with them every week.

He flowed back and dodged the slash. He kicked at the man's knee.

The guy staggered and Ace drove a blow into the man's arm. The asshole dropped the knife, but whirled fast with a growl.

His punch slammed into Ace's gut, driving the air out of him.

"Ace!"

He blocked out Maggie's cry and absorbed the pain. He was not letting this asshole lay hands on her.

Ace snapped his elbow into the guy's face, spun, and followed through with two solid punches.

The guy winced and bent over. Ace rammed his knee

into the guy's face, and the man dropped to the concrete with a low groan.

"Maggie?" Ace asked.

"I'm okay."

Staring down at the guy, Ace pulled out his phone and dialed.

"Yeah," Vander's voice.

"Guy tried to grab Maggie out front of the office. We—"

"Coming. Hang tight."

Ace turned to Maggie. "We'll—"

Her eyes widened. "Ace!"

The blow slammed into the back of his head. The world turned to a dark haze.

Fuck, no. He couldn't lose consciousness. He fought to stay on his feet. He couldn't leave Maggie unprotected.

He heard Maggie cursing, and the sound of a scuffle.

The next thing he realized, he was being dragged along the sidewalk between two guys. The one he'd beaten up was yanking Maggie along. The guy's nose was clearly broken, and he was likely going to get a black eye.

They were led into an alley. Ace pulled in a slow breath. Vander was coming, they just had to hold on a few minutes longer.

"Car's ahead," one guy growled.

Fuck. Ace couldn't let them get him and Maggie in a car. He needed to slow them down.

He swung out and rammed a fist into the guy on the left. The guy grunted. The guy on the right was already reacting.

Ace swiveled and slammed the two guys together. Their foreheads cracked together and they went down.

"Don't move," a deep voice said.

Ace jerked his head up.

The other guy was holding Maggie in front of him, a knife pressed to the delicate underside of her jaw. Fear was alive in her eyes, but she was staying still and calm.

Good girl. Ace met her gaze.

He pulled his phone out, keeping it close to his side. From feel alone, he touched the screen and tapped.

"Hold still, asshole," the man said. "Or I'll cut her up."

Ace looked at the guy. He was sweating, hurting, and nervous.

Ace touched the screen. A high-pitched noise screeched from the phone and he tossed it at the attacker.

The phone hit the man in the head and he staggered.

Maggie jerked free, clamping her hands over her ears.

Ace grabbed her hand. "Run!"

CHAPTER TEN

Maggie clung to Ace's hand as they sprinted down the alley.

They came out on another street, cars driving past, unaware of the drama unfolding. He barely paused, pulling her left.

"Ace, where are we?" There were renovated warehouses and industrial buildings on both sides of the street.

"Not far from the Norcross office. We'll circle back around. Vander will find us."

Gunfire sounded. She screamed, bullets hitting the wall close by.

With a curse, Ace pulled her into another narrow alley.

They ran for what felt like forever, but she heard her attackers following. Soon her lungs were burning.

"Here." He pulled her down yet another alley, past some chain-link fences, and behind some overflowing dumpsters.

"You holding up all right?" he whispered.

She nodded and squeezed his hand.

"Still got your phone?"

"Yes." She pulled it out and told him her code to unlock it.

He tapped in the number and found her contacts. "Vander? Yeah, we're okay. Hiding in an alley. Three assailants. All armed." A pause. "Okay, thanks." He ended the call. "The guys are coming. They've called the police. We just need to sit tight and avoid the bad guys."

"Right." She shivered.

He rubbed her arms. Then they heard voices and they both froze. It seemed like all her senses were enhanced. She smelled rotting food from the dumpsters, and for once her stomach behaved. The sunshine seemed brighter. Were the voices getting closer? She could hear them but she couldn't make out the conversation.

Please just be some passersby.

A strong hand moved down her back. She wasn't alone. She met Ace's gaze. She trusted him. She was still petrified he'd break her heart, but she trusted him.

The voices faded, and a buzzing noise filled the air.

Ace frowned, and peered around the dinged-up dumpster. "Fuck."

But Maggie knew that sound too, and looked up. "It's a drone."

A moment later, the drone maneuvered into the mouth of the alley. Maggie's chest hitched. It looked nothing like her drone. She frowned.

It flew closer.

Ace cursed.

120

"What?" she whispered.

"Military grade. It's got weapons."

Maggie's pulse went haywire. *What?* That's when she spotted the guns mounted on the drone.

This was *insane*.

Ace cursed again, his fingers crushing hers. "It's probably got thermal imaging."

Her eyes widened. "Meaning..."

"It can see us." The drone's weapons opened fire. Bullets pinged off the dumpster and into the brick wall. Maggie screamed.

Ace stood up, grabbed a trash bag out of the dumpster and tossed it into the air.

The drone darted to the side.

Ace yanked her up and pulled her toward the drone.

As it was readjusting, they sprinted under it and out of the alley.

"As fast as you can, Maggie." They ran down the sidewalk. They passed a few bewildered-looking people, but the cars driving past seemed oblivious.

She heard buzzing behind them. "It's coming!"

Ace turned and pulled her into traffic. Cars screeched and horns blared.

A car nearby slammed on its brakes, stopping inches from them.

But Ace didn't slow down.

The drone fired again. Bullets peppered the street and the cars. Screams filled the air. Ace and Maggie ducked behind a stopped car. Ace scanned around. "Come on."

He pulled her up and they sprinted toward a restaurant.

He hit the front door at a run. A few of the people eating at the tables looked up in shock.

"Get down," Ace roared.

Suddenly, the plate glass window shattered in a hail of gunfire.

Diners dropped. He towed Maggie past the startled waitstaff, and through some double doors into a kitchen.

"You can't come back here," spluttered a man in a white coat.

"Back exit," Ace barked. "Now."

Ace's tone got through, as did the sound of more gunfire from the front of the restaurant. The man pointed.

Ace and Maggie raced down a narrow hall and exploded out into the back alley. He pulled her along. A moment later, they crossed another busy street, and Ace shed his jacket and tossed it. He slowed to a walk and tugged her under his arm.

They were just a couple out for a stroll.

Ahead lay the glinting water of the bay, and South Beach Marina, filled with rows of boats. Her heart hammering, every instinct urged her to run as fast as she could.

The buzz of the drone grew louder. Her muscles went stiff.

"Easy," Ace breathed.

They walked into a small park. Thankfully, the patch of grass was empty. She couldn't handle a kid getting hurt.

Ace pulled out her phone, tapping and swiping fast.

"What are you doing?"

"Trying to hack the drone." He had some code up on the screen that looked like gibberish to her.

Casually, he glanced back, and cursed. The buzzing got louder.

"They've spotted us," he bit out.

They broke into a run. The park was mostly just grass, and only a handful of trees, so there weren't many good hiding places.

Suddenly, bullets ripped up the ground behind them.

A scream stuck in Maggie's throat. Ace yanked her sideways and they dove through some bushes.

"Come on," he yelled.

They circled a tree. He paused to tap on the phone again. Bullets hit the tree trunk, and Ace curled his body around hers.

Then he grinned. "See how you like this."

The drone stopped shooting, then flew sideways. He tapped again and it started a crazy, deranged flight path.

Maggie grinned. "You did it!"

Movement caught her eye as three armed men sprinted into the park.

"Ace!"

"Fuck." He grabbed her hand again.

They darted along the grass, shouts echoing behind them.

Ace tugged her through some playground equipment. He paused and tapped on the phone again.

The drone opened fire at the men, and they scattered and dove.

Then suddenly, the drone swiveled and rose higher.

Ace cursed and tapped the phone again. "No. *No*."

"What?"

"I've lost control. There's only so much I can do from a phone."

The drone stabilized and zeroed in on them. Its guns swiveled, and her stomach dropped away.

It fired and Ace leaped on her, taking her to the ground. She felt him jerk and grunt.

"*Ace*."

She looked back over her shoulder.

The drone was flying even closer, the guns pointed right at them. Despair flooded her, squeezing her heart.

Then suddenly, a shot rang out. The drone jerked and then plummeted straight to the ground, crashing into the grass. She watched it bounce.

Chest tight, Maggie looked up... To see Vander standing nearby, feet spread, holding a deadly-looking rifle aimed into the air.

Saxon, Rhys, and Rome were there, too, chasing after the three gunmen. "Ace, thank God," she said. "Vander and the guys are here."

But Ace didn't move. Didn't respond. He was a dead weight on top of her.

"Ace!"

ACE CAME to at the sound of Maggie's frantic voice. He blinked open his eyes and bit back a groan.

Maggie's pale face leaned over him. Saxon was beside her, yanking on Ace's arm. Pain shot through him.

"Easy, Buchanan," Ace muttered.

"Welcome back." Saxon finished wrapping a bandage around Ace's bicep.

"My God." Maggie cupped his cheek. "You got shot!"

"Hey, I'm very alive, *gatinha.*"

There were tears in her eyes.

"No crying, *anjo.*"

She nodded.

Ace sat up and fought back a wave of dizziness. He lifted a hand to the side of his head and realized he must have bumped it on the way down.

He could see that Vander and Rhys had the three attackers on their bellies, hands tied behind their backs.

"Everyone okay?" he asked.

Sunlight glinted off the gold strands in Saxon's hair. The guy came from money, and it was obvious, but he was still a badass.

"Yeah," Saxon replied.

"Except you," Maggie said. "*You* got shot."

"Hunt's on the way," Saxon said. "Rome is getting an X6. We'll take you guys back to the office, and Ryder will meet us there."

Ryder Morgan was Hunt's brother. He was a para-medic, and former Air Force combat medic. He often patched up the Norcross team when they wanted to avoid the hospital.

"He needs a doctor," Maggie insisted.

"It's only a flesh wound," Saxon said.

Maggie sniffed, and Ace watched as anger ignited in her eyes. "Those assholes shot him!"

Uh-oh. "Maggie—"

She leaped up and shot across the grass.

"Shit." Ace got to his feet, ignoring the pain in his arm and a wave of dizziness.

By the time he caught her, she'd kicked one of the attackers in the side.

"You assholes. You think you can just go around shooting people! Trying to kill a pregnant woman."

"Hey, babe, take it easy." Rhys reached for her.

"No!" She kicked another guy.

Ace pulled her close to him with his good arm. "Chill, *gatinha*. It's okay now."

She sucked in a breath, then the fight went out of her.

"I've got you," he said.

She buried her face in his neck. "I was so afraid."

"I know." He hugged her. He'd been terrified while they were running from the drone.

A black X6 pulled up on the street, with Rome's big form behind the wheel.

"Get her back to the office," Vander ordered. "And get that arm checked."

"Oh, your arm," she cried. "Let me go! Did I hurt it?"

"No. Come on, Maggie." He glanced at Vander. "I want the drone."

Vander lifted his chin. "I'll get it."

Ace bundled her into the backseat of the SUV. Rome drove them back to the Norcross office and into the bottom-level parking. Ace led Maggie up into the office area. She lifted a shaky hand to his face.

"*Dios*. What if that drone had—?"

"It didn't." He grabbed her hand and realized it was steady. She was shaken but not falling apart. "My tough *gatinha*."

"I didn't feel tough while we were being chased."

He kissed her nose. "How about when you kicked the bad guys in the ribs?"

Color filled her cheeks. "They made me mad. And they deserved it."

"You do have a temper."

"I heard someone got shot again," a deep, amused voice said.

Ace looked up to see Ryder Morgan coming toward them, wearing a pair of blue scrubs, with a black backpack slung over one broad shoulder. He looked a lot like Hunt, except Hunt looked like the handsome guy-next-door, while Ryder looked like the proverbial bad boy, with his shaggy, brown hair, unshaven jaw, and piercing, green eyes.

"Hey, Ryder."

"Ace," the man replied.

"Just get off at the clinic?" Ryder worked at a free clinic downtown, when he could.

"Yeah." The man's gaze flicked to Maggie.

"I don't think you guys have met. Maggie, this is Ryder Morgan."

"Hunt's brother," she said.

Ryder gave her a slow smile. "Yes, but I'm the better-looking, more-fun Morgan brother."

Ace curled a hand around the back of Maggie's neck.

Ryder's lips twitched at the possessive move, then his

gaze fell to the bandage on Ace's arm. "How about we get you patched up?"

They walked across the space into the Norcross medical room, which Vander kept well stocked.

Ace sat on the bunk while Ryder opened his bag and nabbed a few things off the shelf. Maggie hovered. She looked drained. Ace suspected the stress wouldn't be good for the baby.

Ryder pulled the bloody bandage off Ace's arm.

"Gonna have to have you lose the shirt."

Ace sighed and nodded.

Ryder cut it off him.

Maggie took one look at the bloody wound and clamped a hand over her mouth. She made a strangled sound and raced out of the room.

Shit. Ace tried to lurch after her, but Ryder pushed him down with a hand to the shoulder.

"Sure she can puke without you, brother."

Ace wrinkled his nose.

"She was a helo pilot in the Navy, right?" Ryder started cleaning Ace's wound. "Vander told me she pulled his team out of a hellish situation. Nerves of steel. Would've thought she had a stronger stomach."

"She's pregnant."

Ryder's eyebrows went up. "Baby yours?"

"Yeah."

"Congratulations."

"Yeah, thanks. I think." He blew out a breath. "It wasn't planned. Been a bit of a shock."

"I bet."

Pressure built in Ace's chest. "It doesn't help that I

never planned to have kids and pass my genes down."

Ryder frowned. "I've met your mom and dad. They seem nice."

"Stepdad." Ace's chest was tight, and he realized that this had been stewing from the moment Maggie had told him that she was pregnant. "He adopted me when I was two. But the jerk who contributed biologically was a first-rate asshole. Local drug and crime boss where my mom lived in Rio. Beat her, abused her."

"Shit, Ace."

"She got out when she found out she was pregnant. Met my dad not long after that."

Ryder bandaged up Ace's arm. "It's not all nature, Ace. Nurture plays a part. There are even studies that have been done to show how environment affects our genes, and how they express. You aren't an asshole. I think you'll make a great father."

Maggie staggered back in. "Sorry."

"I hear congratulations are in order," Ryder said with a smile.

She returned it, but it wasn't her usual wattage.

"He's fine," Ryder said. "Flesh wound. Keep it dry for a few days, and here are some pain pills. Especially for the night, to help you sleep."

Ace took them. "Thanks, Ryder."

The paramedic turned to Maggie. "You okay? No injuries?"

She shook her head. "Just a little shaky and a lot mad. Ace shielded me."

"As any good guy would do for his woman and child."

Ace heard the hidden meaning.

ANNA HACKETT

"I just wish we knew who the hell is trying to kill me," she said.

Ace hugged her. "We'll find out."

She nodded.

Suddenly, the door of the medical room flew open. Harlow and Gia raced inside.

"We just heard," Gia said.

"First your car, and now this. Are you all right?" Harlow tugged Maggie away from Ace. "Ace wouldn't let us see you after your Jeep blew up. He said you needed to rest, but enough is enough."

"Haven's on her way from the museum," Gia said. "She's stopping to get pastries from Tartine. Believe me, nothing makes you feel better than a frangipane croissant."

"I'm okay," Maggie said.

"No, you're not." Sofie entered, wearing an elegant, pale-blue dress.

"But you will be after croissants," Gia added.

The women herded Maggie to the couches outside in the main area. She shot Ace a startled look.

Ace wandered out more slowly and when he looked up, he saw Vander and Easton.

"You called in the reinforcements," Ace said to Vander.

"Yeah. Maggie has this deep-seated need to do everything herself. She needs to know that she's not alone."

"I think it's because of her dad. He doesn't give his approval easily, and only on his own terms." How could the man not appreciate the beautiful, vibrant daughter he'd created?

130

"Yeah, seems that parents can mess with the kids," Ryder said as he joined them. "Even if they never raised them."

"Subtle, Morgan," Ace muttered.

Vander met Ace's gaze. Vander was one of the few people who knew about Ace's biological father. "Ryder's right. But there are good parents out there, too. I've got good ones, Ace. Parents who love and support their kids."

"What if I screw up?"

"You will. You just try harder, and you never stop loving them."

Ace grinned. "You'll be a good father one day, Vander."

Vander rolled his eyes. "Shut it, Oliveira, or I'll punch you in your bad arm."

CHAPTER ELEVEN

"Take it easy."

Maggie rushed ahead of him into his house. She hurried to turn lights on. She hadn't relaxed at all since they'd left the office. They'd had an escort home—Rome and Vander following in an X6.

Vander had also told her that they'd have the police do drive-bys, although that made Maggie feel less safe, not more.

At the top of the stairs, she hurried to the couch. "Sit down. I'll get you a drink. And a snack. We missed lunch."

Ace caught her hips. "Maggie."

She sucked in a breath and met his gaze.

"Relax," he said. "I'm okay."

But he could've died. If the bullet had just been a few inches over, it would've caught his chest. She sniffed. If he died...

She was so damn in love with him.

It terrified her.

"Let me look after you," she whispered. "I need to."

Something moved through his gaze. He nodded.

She flitted around in his kitchen and made some sandwiches for them both—thick-cut ham, mustard, cheese. She poured some of his favorite guaraná soda.

"You have a job this afternoon," he reminded her.

"Yes, but I'm in no condition to fly." She sat beside him. "I've already called in a pilot friend of mine, Penny. We were buds from the Navy. It means that I don't make as much, but she's good and safe. She'll take care of my clients, and she flirts outrageously with Gus. He pretends not to like it."

Ace smiled and shoved half a sandwich at her.

She nibbled it.

His phone pinged. "Text from Vander." A scowl flowed over Ace's face. "They questioned the attackers. They aren't talking. They're afraid of whoever hired them."

"Damn. So that leaves us at a dead end." With no idea who was responsible for Adrian Marks' death, or who was trying to kill her.

Ace smiled darkly. "Vander's put Rhys on the case and he's a hell of an investigator. He's digging into Mark's life. And Vander's got feelers out, so it won't be long, and we'll find these assholes."

They finished eating, and Maggie saw Ace shift and wince. "Okay, pain pill for you."

"I'm fine."

"No." She grabbed the pills that Ryder had given him. "Take one, then you need to rest."

He arched a brow.

"You got shot, Ace."

"It's a graze. It's fine."

"Rest." She glared at him.

Then he got a look in his eyes that she didn't quite trust.

"I'll lie down if you lie down with me."

She eyed him. She was pretty sure he was up to something. "All right."

He let her lead him to his bedroom. The room was bright and airy, with gleaming, wooden floors, and a large, wooden bed made up with a cream-and-navy cover. Above the bed, an interesting twist of metal hung on the wall.

Ace lowered the blinds, and when he pulled off the shirt he'd borrowed from a stash at the Norcross office, she almost swallowed her tongue.

He had a lean chest, and abs—not super cut, more toned like a swimmer's. She knew that he ran in the gym regularly. That intriguing tattoo wrapped around his forearm, and God, it suited him.

"Maggie?"

Shaking off her daze, she kicked off her shoes.

"Those jeans won't be comfy." He lay back on the bed and closed his eyes, not even looking at her. "Take them off."

She hesitated, then shoved her jeans down, leaving her in her panties and long-sleeved T-shirt. She lay down beside him. *Hmm*. She wasn't sure she could rest. She was too highly conscious of him lying beside her.

Suddenly, he sprung up, his body covering hers.

"Ace!"

"Now I've got you right where I want you." His fingers skimmed along her jaw, her lips.

"You're supposed to rest."

"I said I'd lie down. I'm lying down." His hands skimmed her body and cupped her breasts.

She couldn't stop her moan.

"These pretty tits are going to get bigger." His eyes gleamed.

"Typical male."

He pushed her shirt up and sucked one lace-covered nipple into his mouth.

Maggie moaned. It felt so good.

"Your arm," she breathed.

"What arm?" He sucked harder.

"*Ace.*" She slid a hand into his silky hair.

"It's fine, Maggie. I know my limits."

She shoved up, pushing him onto his back. "I'm going to make you rest." She ran her hands over his chest. All that smooth, bronze skin, those intriguing muscles.

He arched into her touch. "Well, I guess I'll stay lying flat on my back, if you promise to do exactly what I want."

She narrowed her gaze. That sexy smile fogged her head. She tried to see through this deal of his. The man had trouble written all over him.

"Flat on your back?" she asked.

He nodded.

Heat flooded Maggie's belly. He'd always made her feel so much. She could've lost him today. He could've died, been gone, all because he'd been protecting her.

She swallowed the lump in her throat.

"Hey." He cupped her jaw. "We're both right here, *gatinha*. Alive, breathing, together."

Maggie was done protecting herself, protecting her heart.

If he did end up denting it, it would be better to have had him, for any length of time. To have brilliant, life-filled moments to remember, and share with their child.

"Okay," she whispered.

His sexy eyes flared. "You're all mine now, Maggie."

Her heart skipped a beat. He looked so wicked.

"Take your shirt and panties off," he ordered.

"Why?" she asked warily.

"I want you to climb up here and straddle my face so I can eat that pretty pussy."

Her lower body clenched, blooming with heat.

"You promised," he reminded her.

Licking her lips, she slid off him and onto the bed. She pulled her T-shirt off, then her bra, then she reached down and skimmed her panties down her legs. She was panting, her heart racing.

"Come here," he growled.

She straddled him. She paused, rubbing herself on his sexy abs.

He growled again. "Tease." He gripped her hips. "That's not where I want you."

Maggie moved up, not wanting him to hurt his arm. She sat with her thighs on either side of his head. He shot her a sexy grin, warm breath fanning over her.

Her belly clenched.

"So pretty."

Then his mouth was on her.

Maggie unsuccessfully bit back a moan. Her hands clamped on the headboard, and she needed the anchor as he licked and sucked. His tongue plunged.

A long, low moan tore out of her. Sensation flooded her and it was hard to breathe.

Ace was hungry and he was determined to take his fill of her. His mouth found her clit, sucking hard. She rocked against him.

"Yeah, *gatinha*. Ride my face." His tongue stabbed deep. "You taste like heaven, Maggie."

She couldn't think. She was just a mass of sensation. Ace's hands clamped on her hips, urging her on as he sucked.

Then she fragmented into a thousand, pleasure-soaked shards. She screamed his name.

When she could see and hear and think again, she was on her back on the sheets, a very pleased Ace at her side, smiling at her.

"So fucking beautiful." His hands slid up her thigh. She quivered. "I love how you give me everything in bed, Maggie. Now, I want more."

HIS COCK HURT. He was so damn hard for her.

His *gatinha*.

His Maggie.

Her taste was on his tongue. Ace let his gaze run down her slim body, and pretty pussy, bare except for a patch of dark curls. He slid his hands up her thighs.

"Your arm," she said breathlessly.

It was throbbing a bit. *Hmm.* That meant he needed to get creative.

He slid off the bed, then gripped her and pulled her to the edge. She let out a gasp.

With his good arm doing most of the heavy work, he lifted her.

"*Ace.*"

He quickly crossed the room to his dresser and set her on the edge. He cupped her breast—so high and firm. She was still flushed from her orgasm.

He ran a hand over her body, then slid a finger between her legs and inside her. She moaned, so wet and tight.

He flicked open his jeans.

"Maggie, I got tested the other week." His voice was gritty. "It's part of our regular Norcross health check."

She licked her lips. "And I can't get any more pregnant." She gripped his cock and stroked. "And I'm healthy."

Ace groaned, wrapped a hand around her neck and pulled her forehead to his.

They were close, intimate. It wasn't how he'd ever fucked before. He wrapped his other hand around hers. Together, they guided his cock to her, sliding the head through her damp folds.

Ace thrust deep.

"God, Ace." She threw her head back.

"*Maggie.*" She was tight and hot around his cock.

"You feel so good deep inside me," she murmured.

Ace started moving. He tugged her closer, running

his tongue along the shell of her ear. "Damn, *gatinha*, it was like you were made just for me."

He couldn't stop. He increased the speed and power of his thrusts.

"Yes, Ace." She rubbed against him, taking him, driving back against him.

He angled his hips, hoping each slide would hit where she needed it.

"God, *yes*." Her body clenched on his cock, her nails scraping down his back.

"*Christ*." He powered into her.

One of her hands twisted in his hair. She whimpered, then she was coming.

Fuck. He leaned back so he could see her face, watch as she shuddered through her pleasure.

Sensation hit him like lightning. He grunted, sinking into her soft flesh. He groaned through his release, his muscles straining.

The orgasm was long and hard. He slumped against her, and pressed his lips to the side of her neck.

Maggie tugged on his hair and kissed his mouth.

"Your arm okay?" she murmured.

"*Gatinha*, all I can feel is you. Wet and tight on my cock."

She bit his lip.

Ace slid a hand under her ass and lifted her. He managed to get them to the bed.

"You going to rest now?" she asked.

He grunted and pulled her tight against his side.

ACE MUST HAVE DRIFTED OFF. When he woke again, it was getting dark outside.

And warm lips were moving across his abs.

"*Querida*." His voice was gritty.

"Shush." She wrapped her fingers around his cock and stroked. "I'm driving now."

A groan rumbled out of him. "Yeah?"

"Yeah." She raked her teeth over his hipbone.

He looked at her. She was watching his cock as she pumped him.

"*Gatinha*, you going to suck it or just look at it?"

She bit his stomach this time.

Then she shifted... And closed her mouth over the head of his cock.

She sucked him deep and Ace almost lost it.

He didn't look away, couldn't. She worshiped his cock with a sexy look of delight on her face. She drew back, then bobbed back down, cheeks hollowing.

Sensation sped through him. He'd never had a woman who liked sucking his cock as much as Maggie did. That night they'd spent together, she'd sucked him off three times.

He slid a hand into her hair, his hips bucking. She pulled off and spent some time licking him.

He kept his gaze locked on her face. *Shit.* He wasn't going to last.

She closed her lips tight, sucking hard and moaning.

Enough.

Ace pulled her off him.

"*No*," she cried.

He pulled her up until she straddled him.

Her lips parted. "Yes."

He stroked between her legs, and her body jerked. The head of his cock was lodged just where he wanted it.

Before he could say anything, she sank down.

She took him deep, to the root, and he groaned.

Maggie pressed her hands to his pecs.

"Ride," he ordered.

Her hips moved.

"Get there, Maggie."

She moved faster, taking him deep. Her whimpers urged him on, winding the desire in his gut harder.

She ground down and he moved his hand to find her clit. Her sharp gasp was sweet, sweet music.

Her fingers dug into his chest, her moves turning jerky.

Those liquid-dark eyes met his. "Ace."

"I've got you, *gatinha*. Find it."

Trust and desire on her face, she let go.

Her cries filled the room as she came. He kept working her clit. He slid his hands to her ass and pulled her down hard on his cock.

She moaned again and Ace came. He groaned, his body flooded with pleasure.

Fuck. Shit. He sat up, cupped her face and kissed her.

They came down together, petting and stroking each other.

"I hope your arm's okay."

"I have arms?" he said.

She giggled. A giggle from tough, saucy Maggie Lopez.

"Hungry?" he asked.

She arched a brow. "For food or more sex?"

"Food this time."

"What do you think?"

He squeezed her butt cheek. "That I'd better feed my woman."

Her smile wavered. "Your woman?"

"Yeah." Maggie was his. He just had to get her to trust him enough to believe it.

Her smile came back, brighter than ever. "Yes, you'd better feed me."

CHAPTER TWELVE

M aggie woke with a smile, sprawled in the middle of Ace's bed. She stretched.

The bed was comfy, but the man was missing, though.

She thought of the night and shivered. She felt so good she wanted to get up and dance.

Then thoughts of the drone attack and Ace's injury intruded—dark and ugly. Her stomach did a sickening throb.

She turned her head and spotted crackers and water left on the bedside table. Fighting back a smile, she took her time, nibbling at the crackers. She liked that he was looking out for her. She'd always demanded to do everything for herself. Her mom liked to tell stories about Maggie being a willful toddler, but the few times when she'd really needed support, they hadn't helped her. Her father had forbidden it, and Maggie's mom rarely went against Maggie's dad.

Like when Maggie had needed help securing a loan

for her business. Like the night before her first deployment when she hadn't wanted to be alone. Like when she'd broken an arm during training and needed help for a bit.

If you didn't toe Leo Lopez's line, then you were on your own. But a part of her wanted to trust that Ace wouldn't let her down.

Eventually, Maggie rose and found her panties. She tugged on a T-shirt of Ace's, and it covered her butt. Just.

She went looking for him.

No surprise, she found him in his home office. The screens lit his face in a wash of blue light. He was shirtless—yum—and in jeans.

His head swiveled. "Hey. Feeling all right?"

She nodded. "The crackers helped. Thanks." She slid an arm across his shoulders.

He tugged her onto his lap. His quick, but thorough, kiss left her humming. Then her gaze fell on the bandage on his bicep. She pressed a kiss to it lightly.

He touched a hand to her belly and the look that crossed his face made her face still.

"You're afraid?" she murmured. "Of the baby?"

He blew out a breath. "Afraid I'll do this wrong. Screw it up. Hurt it."

Her heart clenched. "Ace—"

"My dad, he's actually my stepfather."

Maggie heard the dark undertone to his voice. "Okay."

"My biological father is an asshole. He's a criminal drug lord in Rio de Janeiro. He used to beat my mom. And worse. He treated her like a possession, a thing."

Sympathy hit Maggie. "She escaped."

"For me. She was pregnant and afraid that he'd kill us, and that I'd grow up like him if we stayed."

"Ace." Maggie cupped his cheeks, loving the scrape of his stubble. "She got you out. You're a good guy. You served your country, and you help people."

A muscle in his jaw flexed. "I have it in me, Maggie. His blood. I had his temper as a kid, but I learned to lock it down. But sometimes, I look at things and I see ways to skirt the rules. I've done some pretty illegal things."

She snorted. "You mean hacking. You aren't running drugs or selling weapons, Ace. You see ways around things because you're smart and skilled, but that doesn't mean you've got criminal-mastermind leanings."

He stared past her at the computer screen. "My brother, Rodrigo, he OD'd on drugs at a party. He was only fifteen."

And had suffered a brain injury as a result. Maggie's chest tightened. "I'm sorry."

Ace's hand formed a fist on the desk. "He came with me to a party. My mother didn't want him to go, but he really wanted to." A sad smile. "He had a crush on some girl, and I was hooking up with this older girl. I wanted to get laid. I promised I'd take care of him. I was supposed to be looking after him."

Oh, no. So much guilt. So much pain. She stroked his cheek. "It's not your fault, Ace. He made a terrible choice, and he paid a terrible price. But even if you'd been right there, it might still have happened, or if not then, another time."

"I was busy getting laid. Making time with a girl I knew would put out. I left him alone."

"Ace, you can't keep punishing yourself."

"I know he's happy. He likes gaming, he makes models. But he'll never have a career, or fall in love. He hadn't been with a girl before the overdose, and now he never will."

Her heart broke for both Ace and Rodrigo. She hugged him.

"What if I can't keep our baby safe?" he said raggedly.

"Ace, you're keeping me safe."

"You got shot at yesterday."

"And the bad guys are to blame for that. And you got *shot* protecting me." She kissed him softly. "Our baby will have both of us. Not to mention the entire team of badasses you work with and call friends."

He kissed her, but there were shadows still in those eyes.

She realized he'd been carrying around the guilt for a long time. And the shame of who'd fathered him. It was a toxic combination. Maggie made a promise to herself that she'd one day help get him to a point where he wouldn't worry about being a bad father. It would take time, but she'd get him there.

"Sorry." He fiddled with her hair. "Hunt called. He wants me to take you down to the police headquarters. He has some questions for you."

Maggie blew out a breath. "I don't know anything."

"I know, but maybe you know something without realizing it. Hunt's questions might help pry it loose."

She nodded. "You'll come with me?"

"Yes."

They showered, dressed, and had a quick breakfast. Soon, Ace was driving her to police headquarters in the Public Safety Building in Mission Bay.

She looked out the window, at the people on the street. Any of them could be her attackers. She looked up at the sky, her pulse jumping, but she didn't see any killer drones.

Ace parked at police headquarters. He was vigilant as they walked to the front door. They spoke to an officer at reception.

"Detective Morgan is expecting you," the woman said from behind the glass. "I'll have an officer escort you up."

A young man in uniform greeted them and showed them through a door. Ace pressed a hand to Maggie's back as they walked down the corridor.

There was a lot of concrete and glass, and the entire place had a modern feel. She knew the Public Safety Building was quite new, and also housed a fire station and the arson task force.

Their guide led them into a large area covered in open plan desks. Large windows let in light, and there was a row of offices at the back. Phones were ringing and people were talking, or striding through the space with purpose. She spotted Detective Morgan, talking with a man and woman whom she guessed were other detectives.

Maggie was head over heels for Ace, but the woman in her totally acknowledged that Hunter Morgan was hot. If she had to guess, she'd say he'd been the star quarterback at high school—athletic, good at school, and dating the head cheerleader. But now he was all grown-up and it only enhanced his appeal.

Hunt wasn't wearing a jacket, and there was something about a man in a crisp shirt and a shoulder holster. His ex-military background was stamped all over him, in the way he held himself. She saw it in Vander, and the others who worked at Norcross Security, as well.

The other man with him could have answered a casting call for "middle-aged detective", carrying a few extra pounds around the middle, his shirt creased, with a weathered face, and a dash of gray hair at his temples. He had a cynical, resigned look about him.

The woman was younger. Maybe a few years older than Maggie. Her thick, brown hair was in a ponytail, and her white shirt was tucked into black pants, showcasing a fit body. A gun was holstered at her hip.

She elbowed the older man, and he scowled. Hunt smiled, then looked up and spotted Maggie and Ace. He said something to his colleagues, then headed across the room toward them.

The woman caught Maggie's gaze and smiled. If the older guy was middle-aged, jaded cop, this woman was competent, energetic, girl-next-door cop.

"Ace, Maggie." Hunt shook hands with Ace. His green gaze fell on Maggie. "How are you holding up?"

"Well, having someone trying to kill you sucks."

"I'll bet." Hunt waved toward a doorway. "Let's talk in this interview room."

Maggie looked around with interest. It wasn't nearly

as intimidating as in the movies. The room was empty, with the exception of a simple table and chairs.

As she sat, Ace squeezed her shoulder.

"Maggie, Ace is keeping me informed, but I want you to talk me through everything that happened. From the moment these men posing as scientists hired you."

Maggie took the detective through everything. Hunt was methodical, asking her lots of questions. Then the detective sat back in his chair.

"We have the men who attacked you yesterday locked up. They've been charged with assault and I'm pushing for attempted murder. They maintain no knowledge of the drone."

"Bullshit," Ace muttered.

"I know that, but I need this pesky thing called evidence. None of them are talking about whoever hired them." Hunt leaned forward. "Whoever it is, they're afraid of him or her."

Ace bit out a curse. "I'll give them more to be afraid of."

Hunt shot him a thin smile. "I'm a cop, remember? Look, we're tearing these guys' lives apart. They're low-level scum."

"Thugs for hire," Ace said.

Hunt nodded. "They've not got the expertise to organize the drone."

"But they know who did."

"I'm not giving up." Hunt met Maggie's gaze. "I promise you that."

"Thanks, Detective Morgan."

"Call me Hunt. These other Norcross troublemakers do." He nodded at Ace.

Ace took her hand. "We're heading to the Norcross office today."

"I canceled this morning's flights, but Ace, I need to work," she said.

He squeezed her fingers. "I'll help get you sorted out, *gatinha*."

She wasn't alone, and for once in her life, she liked having someone to lean on.

THE NORCROSS SECURITY office was busy when they arrived.

Vander regularly hired a few trusted contractors for certain jobs. Ace nodded at Ben Ryan, a former Navy SEAL, who sometimes helped them out.

"Need a drink or anything?" Ace asked Maggie.

She shook her head. She'd been subdued when they'd left the police station, but she'd rallied on the drive over. Nothing kept Maggie down for long.

"I just need to get some work done. Organize some bookings, and my least favorite job—" she wrinkled her nose "—pay some bills."

He got her set up in his office. Ace followed up on some of his other work—mostly background searches and surveillance. He looked over at the drone that Vander had shot down. It rested on a side worktable.

Time to see what he could get out of this wreck.

Ace fiddled with it, assessing the model and design,

then got out his tools. Using a screwdriver, he opened up the guts of it.

Hmm. He wondered if he could get any data off it. He pulled the chip out, and connected it to his computer.

Whoever was after Maggie must have a decent computer guy on the payroll. Someone had hacked her drone, and someone had been controlling this one.

The chip was damaged, but he managed to pull some data off. He noticed something that came up a few times, buried in the code.

Like a signature.

Ace straightened. Hackers, especially the arrogant ones, sometimes liked to tag their work. Like a graffiti artist.

Over and over, buried in the code, was QU1CK5 1LV3R.

Quicksilver. *Who are you, asshole?*

Ace sat at his computer and opened up a window for the dark web. A few quick searches, and he had some info.

He glanced over and saw Maggie was still busy, frowning at her laptop screen. His gaze traced the slender, sexy line of her neck. It made him want to bite her.

Leaving her to work, he slipped out and headed to Vander's office.

His boss was on the phone, chewing someone out.

"Trucker, you want to keep things easy with me, you quit fucking around with this." A pause. Then Vander's tone darkened. "You want to test me?"

Ace waited in the doorway. Vander could be one

scary motherfucker. His boss glanced over and held up a finger.

"I didn't think so," Vander said. "Good choice. You owe me a marker, Trucker. I'll call it in when I need it."

Vander shoved the cell phone in his pocket.

"Trucker?" Ace said. "As in Eugene 'Trucker' Patterson, head of the Iron Wanderers MC?"

"That's him. Every now and then, Trucker likes to flex his asshole."

The Wanderers were a wild and dangerous motorcycle club. They ran drugs, and were protective of the patch around their clubhouse.

"Whenever Trucker thinks he might like to expand his territory—" Vander leaned against his desk "—I disabuse him of the notion."

Vander had few qualms about bending the law to do the right thing. Norcross Security often operated in the gray to keep people safe. Few people had any clue just how much Vander did behind the scenes—and in the shadows—to keep San Francisco as safe as he could.

"How's Maggie?" Vander asked.

"Cursing as she pays her bills. She's okay, considering."

"You'll get her there, Ace. And we will find whoever is after her."

Ace nodded. "I have a lead. I got something off the drone you toasted. Did you have to shoot it to smithereens?"

"I was more interested in saving yours and Maggie's asses at the time."

"Right. The code on it has got a hacker's tag in it.

Quicksilver. There's not much on him, but I found a hacker out of New York that uses that name."

Vander nodded, his gaze narrowing. "Let me make some calls. Maverick Rivera and his woman, Remi, could help."

Ace and Vander had helped out Mav and Remi in New York. Mav was a tech billionaire, and Remi a white-hat hacker called Rogue Angel.

"I was thinking that," Ace said.

"And I'll talk to Hawke."

Ace lifted his chin. Killian Hawke was the shadowy, lethal owner of Sentinel Security, and Remi's boss. He'd also helped during Mav and Remi's thing. His security company also did a lot of cybersecurity.

"Let me know if they know this guy," Ace said.

"On it. I've got yours and Maggie's backs, Ace."

"Thanks, Vander."

As Ace headed to his office, he heard Maggie's throaty laugh. He found Saxon with her, one hip hitched on the desk beside her.

"Hey, Ace," Saxon said.

Ace lifted his hand.

"You taking good care of our girl?" the man asked.

Ace glanced at Maggie and saw her cheeks heat. He grinned. "I am. *Very* good care."

Saxon rolled his eyes, then patted Maggie's shoulder. "You need anything, you let me know." He rose, letting his suit jacket fall back into place. "Oh, and Gia's planning something, so brace."

Maggie blinked. "Planning what?"

"No clue, but I know she's worried about you. And

when my woman puts her mind onto anything, watch out. She wants to do something to cheer you up."

Vander appeared in the doorway as Saxon left. His face was serious.

"We have a video call with Killian. He's got something for us."

Ace's pulse jumped. "Already?"

Vander nodded. "Pull him up."

Maggie wheeled her chair closer to Ace's, while he sat and tapped the keyboard. Vander stood behind them.

A second later, a man's face appeared on the screen.

Killian Hawke was lean, had a hawkish face, and black hair. His dark eyes looked sharp. In fact, that was the word that sprung to mind looking at him: sharp. Like a knife ready to cut at the right moment.

"Vander, Ace," Killian said.

Beside Ace, Maggie's eyes widened. Hawke also had a voice Ace was sure drove the women wild.

"Killian." Ace nodded at Maggie. "This is Maggie Lopez."

"Ms. Lopez. I'm sorry to hear about your troubles."

"Thanks. And it's Maggie."

"I received information from Vander that you think Quicksilver is involved. He's a punk. Real name is Joseph Cantor, twenty-three, originally from London. He's out to cause anarchy and end the oppression. Believes everyone should be able to do exactly as they please, laws be damned."

"Sounds charming," Maggie said.

"He sometimes hires out. Big jobs, small jobs, he doesn't care. He just takes what appeals to his sense of chaos." Killian frowned. "That said, I've never heard of him agreeing to murder before. He's not afraid to break the law, but he prefers jobs that don't involve a life sentence."

"Any idea how to track him down?" Vander asked.

"I'll send you the file my team has on him." Killian looked up, meeting Vander's gaze. "I can tell you that the guy loves cotton candy. Addicted to the stuff. If he's in San Francisco, he'll be buying. A lot of it."

Maggie blinked and gave a hiccupping laugh. "One of my would-be killers likes cotton candy?"

Ace rubbed her back.

"There are a few hackers that he might associate with on the West Coast," Killian continued. "Kevin Farrell and Nick Chan."

Ace's gut hardened. "I know them. They go by Cowboy and Lone Wolf."

"We might need to pay them a visit," Vander drawled.

"One more thing," Killian said. "Vander sent me your photograph of the bomber."

"It's not a great shot," Ace said.

"I can ID him," Killian said.

Both Ace and Vander leaned forward.

"Who is he?" Ace barked.

"A dirtbag by the name of Ross Booker. He's from New Jersey. He and Quicksilver have worked together before. Bank robbery and an arson attack."

Ace glanced at Vander. Finally, a break.

"Thanks, Killian," Vander said. "This is just what we needed."

"Anytime, Vander." Killian smiled at Maggie. "Stay safe." The screen went blank.

"We track down Quicksilver and Booker, and shut them down," Ace said. "Find out who's giving their orders."

"Yeah, we want whoever is pulling the strings." Vander rapped his knuckles on the desk. "Let's go and visit Farrell and Chan, Ace."

"I have a tour this afternoon." Maggie looked at her watch. "In just under two hours."

"I'll line up Rhys to stay with you, while Ace and I run these hackers down," Vander said.

Ace kissed the top of her head. "Rhys will take good care of you."

She grabbed his hand. "You be careful, too."

CHAPTER THIRTEEN

R hys pulled his hot, sleek Mercedes GT in at her landing pad.

The Norcross men sure liked their sexy cars.

"Thanks for babysitting, Rhys," Maggie said.

He flashed her a smile and she fought back a giddy sigh. Rhys Norcross was gorgeous. He looked like a rock star—shaggy dark hair, handsome face, tattoos, and a twinkle in his sexy, dark eyes.

Maggie saw a woman nearby do a double-take and give him a long, hungry look.

As they walked toward her office, she spotted Gus getting Hetty prepped and waved. He jerked his head and shot Rhys an unhappy glare. She led Rhys into the office.

"Make yourself at home. You're welcome to make a coffee."

He lifted his chin, dropped onto the couch, and pulled out a tablet.

Maggie checked her emails. The clients due for the

tour of the Bay were a vacationing family—parents and two young boys.

But her thoughts turned to Ace and Vander. She worried her bottom lip. Going to question the hackers shouldn't be dangerous, but worry still made her nerves dance.

"Maggie?"

She jerked her head up and saw Rhys looking at her.

"It's going to be fine."

She nodded. "I'm worried about Ace and Vander."

Rhys had a sexy laugh, too. Haven was a lucky woman.

"Don't. Those two can handle themselves."

"I'm sure Vander could single-handedly defeat a small army," Maggie said.

"Sure, but don't let the geek fool you. Ace is trained and capable. They'll be fine."

She blew out a breath. She just hated waiting, but thankfully the Ellis family arrived to distract her. The parents were lovely, and the kids delightful. The older boy was about ten, and bouncing with eagerness for his first helicopter ride. The younger boy said he was excited, but was unsuccessfully hiding his nerves.

As the family climbed into Hetty, Maggie crouched. "There's nothing to be worried about, big guy."

The boy gave her a tentative nod. "Is it loud?"

"Well, Hetty is pretty noisy."

"Hetty?"

Maggie patted the side of the helicopter. "The name of my girl here."

The little boy's face perked up. "She has a name?"

"She sure does. Henrietta, but I call her Hetty for short. And I have a nifty headset for you to wear."

He shot her a small smile. "Cool."

She got everyone settled, and Rhys sprawled in the copilot seat beside her, looking very comfortable. She wasn't surprised. He was former Ghost Ops. He'd probably lost count of how many times he'd flown in a helicopter.

Finally, they lifted off, and she watched the boys glued to the side window, their excitement obvious. She did a loop over the Bay, which she knew like the back of her hand. She spoke into her headset, giving a little commentary on the landmarks. When they passed close to the Golden Gate Recreational Area and Muir Woods, she stared at the trees, her stomach hard.

But she shook it off. It was easy to do when every time she glanced back, the boys were bouncing in their seats and peppering their parents with questions.

When they finally landed back on the landing pad, the boys had huge grins and flushed faces.

Even Rhys, born and raised in San Francisco, looked like he'd had a good time.

Once they were all out of the helo, she turned Hetty over to Gus, then waved the family off.

"You look like you enjoyed the ride," she said to Rhys.

"Babe, it's nice to be in a helo and not be clutching an assault rifle, preparing to fast rope out of it."

She smiled. "I guess." Then her smile faded. "Any news from Vander?"

Rhys shook his head, a dark lock of his hair falling over his forehead. "They'll be fine. Just relax." He scanned the area, reminding her that he was on duty. "Let's get back inside."

She led the way, chewing on her lip again. *Be okay, Ace.*

VANDER PULLED the X6 up near the rundown apartment building in the Tenderloin.

Ace scanned it through the window. "Nice."

The street was littered with trash, and someone had dumped a shag rug on the corner, along with a dismantled bike frame.

As they exited the SUV, Vander checked his Glock 22, then strode inside. The entry door lock was broken. An enterprising artist had left a picture of a dick and balls spray-painted on the wall.

Better and better. Something crunched under Ace's boots, and he didn't bother to look down.

Vander took the stairs. On the second floor, he headed down a hall that had worn, dirty carpet, and smelled faintly of wet dog.

A bottle blonde dressed in a short, black dress leaned in one of the doorways.

Her gaze sharpened on Ace, then Vander.

"Hey boys, interested in a blow job? I usually charge thirty bucks, but for you fine specimens, I'll do it for twenty."

Vander glanced her way. "No."

She eyed him, then her face shut down, and she

slipped back into her apartment. The door closed with a sharp bang.

Vander stopped at a door farther down the hall.

"Let me knock," Ace said. "So, you don't make them crap themselves."

Vander stepped out of view and Ace rapped his fist on the wood.

Silence, then footsteps. "Who is it?" a voice called through the door.

"Oliveira."

Frenzied whispers. Then the door opened a few inches.

"Hey, Ace, long time no see," the man said.

Kevin "Cowboy" Farrell was tall, and so skinny he looked ill. He had pale skin, and a mop of shaggy hair in a dishwater brown.

The smell of weed wafted out of the apartment. Kevin looked like he hadn't showered in a few days.

"Hi, Kev. Need to talk to you and Nick."

"Kind of busy, man. Can you come back another day?"

"No."

Kevin frowned. "Dude, we're busy."

"Fuck off!" a voice shouted from inside.

That would be Nick "Lone Wolf" Chan. Kevin moved to close the door when Vander stepped in, and shoved his boot against it.

Kevin stared at Vander like a tiger had just appeared. His eyes went comically wide.

"N-N-Norcross."

"Tell whoever it is to fuck off," Chan shouted again.

Vander shoved open the door and strode in. Kevin stumbled back.

The apartment was crappy, dark, and dirty.

They found Nick Chan seated behind two monitors set up on a rickety table made of scarred wood. The table was cheap, but the screens and computer were top-of-the-line.

As Vander bore down on Nick, the idiot finally tore his gaze from the screens.

His dark eyes went wider than Kevin's.

Nick had ruler-straight, black hair, with a streak of blue through it. "Norcross," he stuttered.

Vander put his boot to the chair, right between Nick's legs and kicked. The chair and Nick fell backward and smacked against the floor.

"Now," Vander said. "We have a few questions for you."

Ace hid his laugh behind a cough.

Nick scrambled to his feet, and both men stood side-by-side, like naughty kids sent to see the school principal.

"Quicksilver," Vander said.

Kevin jerked and Nick blinked rapidly.

"Never heard of him," Nick said.

Ace groaned. "Listen up, you morons, we work in security and investigations. We can tell when people are lying."

Vander's tone dipped to frigid levels. "So don't lie to me."

Both hackers swallowed.

"He said he was in town," Nick said. "We game online sometimes, but we haven't seen him."

Ace narrowed his gaze. "You know why he's here?"

"Got a big job," Kevin blurted.

Nick shot him a dirty look.

"A big job killing a woman?" Ace said silkily. "*My* woman?"

Both hackers stiffened.

"Quicksilver didn't say nothing about killing no one," Kevin said.

Vander circled the apartment.

Kevin and Nick watched him warily.

"You know where Quicksilver might stay?" Ace asked.

The men shook their heads, still watching Vander. Vander walked into the tiny kitchen. Ace arched his head and saw the sink was overflowing with dirty plates. The place was a pigsty.

There was a rustling sound, and then Vander came back. He was using a latex glove to hold up some plastic.

"Care to explain this?" Vander asked.

Ace stared at the wrapper...from a package of cotton candy.

"Your trash can is full of these," Vander continued.

Ace thought of Maggie running from her drone, waking screaming from her nightmare, getting shot at by the second drone.

She was in danger and it was his job to protect her. The tight ball in his chest grew bigger. These two idiots were standing in his way.

Ace exploded. He shoved Kevin, who tripped and fell with a squawk.

Then Ace swiveled and shoved Nick against the wall,

his forearm to the hacker's throat. Nick scratched at Ace's arm and made a gurgling sound.

"Where the fuck is Quicksilver?" Ace asked.

Nick's eyes flared, but he stayed silent.

"He's working for the fucker who's trying to kill my woman. My pregnant woman."

Nick blanched. Kevin, still on the floor, made a wheezing sound.

"Tell him," Vander ordered.

"He's staying here," Nick choked out. "He went out for cigarettes and to get some more of that fucking cotton candy."

Ace put more pressure on Nick's throat and his eyes bulged. "Good choice."

"Why's the front door open?" a British-accented voice called out. A young man strolled in, stuffing pink cotton candy in his mouth. He had curly brown hair, a large nose, and large, brown eyes.

When he saw Ace and Vander, he froze, dropped the candy, and ran.

But Vander was faster.

Ace didn't even see Vander move. He lunged after Quicksilver and, a second later, dragged the twisting, cursing hacker back inside.

He tossed Quicksilver on the couch.

"Sit and don't move," Vander warned.

Ace released Nick.

Quicksilver wiped a hand across his mouth. He wore a large, gray hoodie and blinked rapidly.

"You don't want to mess with me, bastards," Quicksilver yelled. "I have friends who will fuck you up."

Kevin and Nick desperately shook their heads, trying to get Quicksilver to shut up.

Vander shifted closer. "You know who I am?"

"Don't care if you're the bloody Queen."

Vander crouched in front of Quicksilver. "My name is Vander Norcross."

Quicksilver clamped his mouth shut.

"I'm guessing you do know who I am. You're in my city now, and I expect you to answer my friend's questions."

Quicksilver's face rippled, he glanced at Ace, but he didn't say anything.

Ace stepped forward. "We shot your drone down."

Quicksilver surged up, but Vander pushed him back down on the couch.

"That bloody drone took me *forever* to put together. The programming was a piece of art. I can't believe you wrecked it."

"It was fucking firing on me and my woman," Ace said.

The hacker went pale. "No. It wasn't armed."

Ace pointed to the bandage on his arm. "I've got the flesh wound to prove it was, asshole."

Quicksilver swallowed convulsively. "He never said anything about shooting at anyone. I programmed it for him, but it was just supposed to follow her, chase her. Mess with her a bit."

"Who is *he*?" Ace asked, his voice low and vibrating with rage.

"Spiner. Paul Spiner."

A muscle ticked in Ace's jaw. "Paul Spiner is a sixty-six-year-old professor at the University of San Francisco."

Quicksilver's brow creased. "No, that ain't right. Dude is younger."

"Around forty?" Ace asked. "Brown hair, blue eyes."

"Yeah." Quicksilver wiped a hand across his mouth. "He paid well. Flew me out here and it all sounded fun."

"To terrorize a woman?" Vander's tone dropped temperature several degrees.

Quicksilver licked his lip. "She's his ex. Said she's a real bitch."

Ace exploded. He grabbed the front of Quicksilver's shirt and yanked him up. He spun the man and slammed him into the table. The monitors rocked.

"He barely knows her," Ace said. "She's *my* woman, and pregnant with my baby."

"Oh, fuck." Quicksilver was breathing hard. "I didn't know. I didn't know."

"Your drone shot at her. Someone put a fucking bomb in her car."

Quicksilver started sweating. "I didn't know."

Ace shoved him again and the guy cried out.

"Ace," Vander said.

Ace released the man. "Where do we find this Spiner?"

"I met him at an office. A shitty place in a strip mall." Quicksilver rattled off the address.

"And do you know where Ross Booker is?" Vander asked.

Quicksilver closed his eyes. "Shit. Booker came out

with me from New York. You said there was a bomb in her car?"

"Yes," Ace said.

"Look, Booker is a decent guy—"

Ace shifted and Quicksilver cut off.

"He nearly killed an innocent woman," Ace said. "Where. Is. He?"

Quicksilver blew out a shaky breath. "He's staying in a cheap motel by the airport. The Cozy Inn."

"I suggest you head back to New York, Quicksilver," Vander said. "And don't come back to San Francisco again."

The man's head bobbed.

Vander pointed at Kevin and Nick. "And I'll be watching you two."

They both nodded.

Ace and Vander strode out. Once they were out of the apartment building, Ace pulled in a few deep breaths.

"I need to call Hunt in on this," Vander said.

Ace nodded.

Back in the X6, Ace listened as Vander talked to Hunt.

"Good. We'll meet you there." Vander paused. "Yeah, yeah, we won't make a mess." He made a sound. "And yeah, I'll owe you. Again."

Vander ended the call and started the engine. "Hunt's sending cops to pick up Booker at the motel. He'll meet us at Fake Spiner's office."

"Good."

Vander drove fast, and soon, they were pulling in at the strip mall in Diamond Heights. They screeched to a stop, just as an unmarked Dodge Charger pulled up, along with a police car.

Hunt climbed out of the Charger and waved. Two uniforms got out of the other car and joined him.

Ace studied the office.

Cityscape Holdings.

"Let's go in," Hunt said.

They knocked. The front doors were locked, and there was no answer. They peered in through the smoky glass.

"No one inside." Hunt nodded at the uniforms. "Break it down."

"Wait." Vander pulled out a set of lock picks. It took him thirty seconds, and the door swung open.

The office inside was empty.

The uniforms cleared the rooms. "No one here, Detective."

Ace, Vander, and Hunt checked the two offices. The desks were empty, and there were a few loose papers on the floor. The filing cabinet doors hung open.

Ace studied the cords by the desks. "There were computers here."

"They left in a hurry." Hunt frowned.

Fuck. Ace kicked the desk. Fake Spiner was long gone, and they still had no idea who he really was.

"We'll pull Cityscape Holdings apart," Vander said. "We're not giving up."

They weren't giving up, but Maggie still wasn't safe.

CHAPTER FOURTEEN

Maggie paced Ace's living room. *Where was he?*

"Babe," Rhys said. "Chill."

She glared at him. He was sprawled on the couch, looking sexy and unconcerned. He was flicking through channels on the television.

"I can't chill."

"I told you that Ace and Vander are fine. They'll be here soon."

She blew out a breath. He'd also told her that they'd found something, and that Ace would share when he got here.

She heard the front door and her pulse jumped.

"See," Rhys said.

She rolled her eyes at him. Ace and Vander appeared, and both of them looked perfectly normal, no injuries.

Ace moved straight to Maggie and hugged her. She saw Vander flick a finger at his brother.

"Why don't you sit down, *gatinha*?"

Her gut cramped. "It's bad."

"No. It's just not where I'd like it to be."

She dropped down by Rhys. Ace sat on the coffee table in front of her and took her hands. Vander stayed standing, his hands on his hips.

"We visited Farrell and Chan, the local hackers. Quicksilver was staying with them."

Rhys leaned back. "Is he still breathing?"

"Yes," Ace said. "He gave us Booker, the bomber. He's in police custody."

Maggie gasped and squeezed Ace's fingers. "Okay. So that's good. He can't hurt anyone else."

"Quicksilver also told us that Spiner is the one giving the orders. Or rather the fake Spiner. He gave us an address of an office where he met with the guy."

Maggie swallowed. "Go on."

"Vander and I checked it out with Hunt. The guy was long gone, and had cleaned the place out."

That explained the frustration she felt from Ace. "Oh, so do you think he's left town?" God, she hoped so.

"Maybe," Vander said. "But I don't make decisions based on hope."

"The office was for Cityscape Holdings. I've been doing some digging. It's a property development firm. They bought some land in Dogpatch where they're building luxury apartments. It's owned by this man, Davis Haye." Ace held up his tablet.

"That's *him*." Maggie jolted. "That's Fake Spiner."

"The guy sunk his life savings into the project. He brought in investors and he borrowed deep."

"Like bottom of the ocean deep," Vander said.

"And?" she prompted.

Vander shifted. "And he cut corners to save costs. Last week, the city building inspector didn't pass the current work on the development."

"Adrian Marks," she whispered.

"Right," Ace said. "Witnesses saw Haye and Marks arguing. Haye made threats."

"And apparently Haye considers himself very smart and cunning." Vander's tone said the opposite. "He's always bragging about his latest moneymaking schemes, about how clever he is. But with everything sunk in this building project, he was desperate."

"So, he concocted a convoluted scheme to get Marks alone, and no doubt try to convince the guy to change his report," Ace continued. "I assume Marks didn't budge."

"So Haye killed him." She entwined her fingers with Ace's. "And he used me as part of this complicated coverup."

"My guess is he had one of his thugs drive out to meet them at Muir Woods."

"They were no doubt hoping Maggie wouldn't notice anything amiss," Rhys added.

"And Haye wasn't expecting Maggie to put the drone up," Ace added.

She nodded. "That's why he got agitated."

"And after he failed to get his hands on your footage, he decided the best plan was to eliminate you," Vander said. "He hired Quicksilver and Booker. Out-of-towners who couldn't be linked back to him."

She pressed a hand to her cheek. "God."

"He had millions at stake," Ace said. "And he was losing everything. His wife also left him."

"So, he figured he'd just *kill* me?" Maggie shook her head. "Jesus, some people suck."

Ace pulled her to his chest. "We'll find Haye, and until then, we'll keep you protected."

"But it's likely he's run, right? Why would he stay here?"

A groove appeared in Ace's brow. "Until I have proof, I'm not buying it."

"I guess I should head out," Vander said.

"Actually, you should stay," Rhys said.

Vander raised a brow at his brother. "Oh, is this your house now?"

Rhys smiled his rock-star grin. "No, Haven just texted me. She's on her way over with Gia and the gang." He glanced at Maggie. "They wanted to do something to cheer you up."

"Cheer me up?"

"Yeah. Now usually Gia's idea of cheering someone up involves cocktails and a party. In these circumstances —" he gestured at Maggie's stomach "—she's been forced to get creative."

"Well, Gia isn't short on creativity," Vander said. "Are they bringing food?"

"Yep," Rhys answered.

"Good." Vander dropped into an armchair.

"I guess we're having a party." Ace smiled.

About thirty minutes later, the extended Norcross gang descended.

Gia bustled in, holding a stack of shopping bags. Haven, Harlow, and Sofie brought in trays of food. Easton, Rome, and Saxon followed with drinks.

Maggie got hugs from everyone.

"It's a night to relax, unwind, and have a laugh." Gia patted Maggie's arm. "We are all-too-aware of how it feels to be in your position, and you shouldn't be stressed right now."

Unruly tears threatened. "Crap, Gia, don't make me cry."

"Get some food. You're eating for two now."

"The baby is the size of a seed, so I'm not sure I can justify doubling my plate."

"Pfft." Gia served up a creamy pasta and handed it over.

The men ate, drank, and talked work, sports, and cars.

"Here." Sofie delivered a drink topped with greenery to Maggie. "A virgin mint julep."

Across the room, she saw Ace smiling at her. This was...nice.

She ate more and watched him. She wanted this, the two of them together, hanging with their friends.

But did he want her enough? He seemed to have no problems with the bachelor life. God, what if he felt trapped?

"Okay?" He appeared, squeezing the back of her neck.

She nodded quickly.

After they'd all eaten, Gia stood. "All right, it's time for the gifts. Mostly, the men handed over money and let us ladies do our thing."

"Thank God," Vander muttered.

"I helped," Rhys said.

"You did." Haven kissed him noisily.

"You didn't have to do this." Maggie settled on the couch and Ace perched on the arm beside her.

Gia handed over the shopping bags. "Yes, we did. Besides, it was fun."

Maggie pulled open the first bag and lifted out the clothes inside.

"Oh." A huge jolt hit her. "Oh, God."

It was a tiny onesie in a buttery-cream color. On the front of it was a picture of a bar loading, like from a computer program. Under the image it said, "Warning: diaper loading."

Ace chuckled, and then she held it up to the others. More laughter filled the room.

Maggie stroked the soft fabric, trying to imagine a little person small enough to fit inside it.

The next onesie was gray, and had a picture of glasses on it with "Geek in training" written underneath.

"Funny," Ace said.

"Look at the next one," Rhys urged. "I picked it."

Maggie did. It said, "My daddy is a geek, but I'm living proof he scored at least once."

Maggie snort-laughed and Ace groaned.

Rhys looked smug. "Good, huh?"

"Thank you." Maggie looked around the room. "These are awesome."

There were also cute pacifiers, a set of tiny shoes, and an ultrasoft blanket.

"We'll have a big baby shower bash closer to your due date," Gia said. "I just wanted to do a little something fun, in the middle of the not-so-fun."

Maggie leaned over and hugged Gia. "Thank you so much."

"You're not alone," Gia whispered.

The gathering wound down, and everybody finally headed home.

When Maggie closed the front door and returned, she found Ace fingering the onesies.

"Makes it a little more real," she said.

He lifted his chin. "Makes me realize I can't let up on keeping you safe."

Her heart clenched and she moved over to him. "It's not all your responsibility. We're in this together, Oliveira."

He ran a hand along her cheekbone.

"How about if I take my baby daddy to bed?" she murmured. "And do naughty things to him?"

His lips twitched. "Hmm, let me think about it... Yes."

She kissed him. Right there and then, it was just the two of them. For a little while, they'd shut out the world.

ACE WATCHED Maggie brushing her teeth in his bathroom and grinned.

Damn, he liked seeing her there. They'd showered, and she was just wearing a towel wrapped around herself. It gave him ideas.

A cell phone started ringing in the bedroom. She met his gaze in the mirror. "That's mine," she mumbled around her toothbrush. "Can you grab it for me?"

When he returned with it, she'd just finished rinsing.

She snatched the phone with a smile. "Thanks."

Ace took the opportunity to slide a hand under her towel and squeeze her ass cheek.

She smacked his arm, but was grinning. Then she thumbed the phone and held it up on speaker. "Hi, Mom."

Mom? Shit. He pulled his hand back.

"Sweetie, where are you?" Her mother's voice came through loud and concerned.

Maggie frowned. "Mom, what do you—?"

"Magdalena?" Her father's deep baritone. "We're at your apartment and you didn't answer our knocks."

"We wanted to surprise you," her mother said.

Maggie closed her eyes and Ace stroked a hand down her back.

"We were worried," her mother continued. "So, we spoke with those lovely neighbors of yours. The Paulsons. They said you haven't been home for *days.*"

"And they told us that your apartment was broken into and your Jeep exploded out on the street," her father growled.

A sob came across the line, and Ace assumed Mrs. Lopez was crying.

"Mom, Dad, I'm fine. I didn't want you to worry."

"Where are you, Magdalena?" her dad asked.

"I'm staying with a friend."

There was a pause.

"A man?" Her father sounded like he tasted something bad.

"Look, why don't—"

"We want to see you Maggie," her mother insisted.

"We came all the way up here," her father added.

Without even calling her or planning ahead. Ace saw Maggie rub her temple.

"Why don't we meet up for breakfast," Maggie said. "At Home Plate. Mom, it's one of your favorites." Maggie looked over at Ace and he nodded.

"All right," her mother said. "You're sure you're okay?"

"Yes."

"Then we'll see you soon, sweetie."

"Sorry." Maggie winced. "I should've called them, but I didn't want them to worry, and I didn't need the added drama right now. Just drop me at Home Plate and I'll call you when I'm done."

"Oh, no." Ace gripped her hips. "I'm coming to this breakfast."

Emotions flitted across her face. "Okay." She didn't sound thrilled.

"And if your father says one thing to you that I don't like, we're leaving."

"Ace—"

He kissed the tip of her nose. "No buts. Now get some clothes on that sweet butt of yours before I need to fondle it some more."

That got a smile out of her, but he still saw the shadows in her eyes.

Ace hated his biological father. He'd never met him, never wanted to, but he had researched the hell out of him. It was a clear-cut case of Ace wanting nothing to do with the man who contributed his DNA.

But Maggie's relationship with her father was a more nuanced thing. It was clear she loved him, even when he left her bruised.

Soon they were driving to Home Plate, not far from her apartment. Ace snagged a parking spot close by, and they walked into the old-school-style diner, his hand on Maggie's lower back.

A couple stood up at one of the long, wooden tables at the back, and instantly, he knew it was her parents.

Maggie had her father's height, dark hair, and body, but her mother's face.

Beside him, he felt Maggie steeling herself.

"Mom, Dad." She hugged them both. "This is Ace. Ace Oliveira."

He met their curious gazes. Kiki Lopez was eyeing him with interest, but Leo Lopez didn't bother to hide his disapproval.

Luckily, Ace didn't scare easily.

"It's nice to meet you." Ace held out a chair for Maggie.

They sat and a young server hurried over. Maggie was a little pale, and just ordered a croissant. Ace ordered pancakes.

"What happened to that crap Jeep of yours?" her father barked. "I told you that you needed a new car years ago."

Maggie lifted her chin. "Someone put a bomb in it."

Her parents' mouths dropped open.

Ace curled a hand at the back of her neck. "There's a police investigation. We can't discuss the details."

"Maggie." Her mother reached across the table and grabbed her hand.

"I'm staying with Ace. The guys at Norcross are taking good care of me."

Leo sat back in his chair. "You work for Norcross?"

Ace nodded.

"Oh." Kiki sipped water and sent a worried glance at her husband.

"I've been telling her that she shouldn't be working at that place. It's too dangerous."

Ace arched a brow. "Maggie is a hell of a pilot. She is an indispensable part of the Norcross team, and we would never put her in any unnecessary danger."

Leo grunted. "And yet someone's putting bombs in her car."

"Which has nothing to do with Norcross," Maggie said.

The older man grunted.

Thankfully, their food arrived.

"You can't say...more about who blew up your SUV?" Her mother was clearly worried.

"No, Mom, the police are investigating."

"The person responsible has been arrested," Ace told them. "But whoever gave the order is still on the loose."

"Come home with us," her father said. "You'll be safer out of San Francisco."

Ace tensed. He didn't want Maggie anywhere out of his sight.

Maggie shook her head. "I can't, Dad. I have work. I have bills and loans to pay."

"You should never have gone into all that debt."

Kiki got a pinched look. She was clearly bracing for an argument.

Maggie set her knife down. "Dad—"

"I ran a successful business for years," he said. "I know—"

"Yes, you know. You have to be right *all* the time, and have things all your way."

Leo's face turned red. "Don't talk to me that way. I'm your father, and you'll show me respect."

"If you don't respect my decisions, I'll talk to you however I need to."

"Maggie's good at what she does," Ace said. "She's put together an excellent business, and like I said, she's a hell of a pilot. You should be proud."

"You stay out of this," her father barked.

"Dad," Maggie snapped. "Do *not* talk to him that way."

Ace squeezed her neck again. Under the table, she gripped his thigh.

"Maggie." Kiki tried to be the peacemaker. She'd probably had lots of practice. "We're just worried about you. Please think about coming home with us."

"Thanks, Mom, but I'm staying with Ace. I'm safe. I promise." Suddenly, she went pale.

"Here." Ace held out a glass of water and stroked her back.

"Thanks." She shot him a wan smile and sipped the water.

Her parents frowned at her.

"Sweetie, are you sick?" her mother asked.

Maggie met Ace's gaze. He nodded. He figured it was best to rip the bandage off.

She straightened her shoulders. "No, I'm pregnant."

Silence fell across the table.

Kiki blinked rapidly. Leo didn't blink at all. He looked frozen.

Then Maggie's father set his knife and fork down. He looked at Ace. "You got my daughter pregnant?"

"She's having my baby, yes."

Mmm, saying that didn't make him break out in a sweat quite as much as it had a few days ago.

Leo fell worryingly silent, and Kiki was watching him, as though he were a ticking bomb.

Kiki finally took Maggie's hand. "This is a surprise."

"It wasn't planned," Maggie said. "We're both still getting used to the idea, ourselves."

"When are you getting married?" her father demanded.

"Dad, it isn't the Dark Ages. You don't have to be married to have a child anymore."

Leo went red again. "No child of *mine* is having a baby out of wedlock."

"Wedlock?" Maggie said. "Who even uses that word?"

Ace felt his anger swelling.

"I do," Leo growled.

Maggie rolled her eyes. "I'm not a child, Dad. I'm an adult. Fully grown."

"What you are is a silly girl, with mountains of debt, and now unwed and pregnant. A total failure."

Maggie jerked like he'd hit her. Ace had had enough.

He threw his napkin down, stood, and pulled Maggie up with him.

"That's enough. You should be proud of Maggie's accomplishments. She achieved them all by herself, with no help from you. And you should celebrate your grand-child, and know that Maggie—smart, sassy, lively Maggie —will make a wonderful mother."

She looked at him, her lips parted. There were tears shimmering in her eyes.

Ace took her hand. "A brilliant mother, who'll help me be the father this child deserves."

Ace pinned her parents with a hard stare. Kiki had tears in her eyes, Leo's jaw was working.

"Not a father like you, where love and approval are conditional on following your orders." Ace tugged Maggie's hand. "We're leaving, *gatinha*."

CHAPTER FIFTEEN

M aggie smiled as she finished up her day. She'd had several flights today, and they'd all gone smoothly.

There'd been no sign of Davis Haye. No creepy guys watching her. No killer drones.

Finally, it seemed that this nightmare was over. She felt like a weight was slowly lifting off her shoulders.

Ace sat sprawled in her desk chair. It would mean that she'd lose her sexy bodyguard. She smoothed her hair back. And she'd have to move back into her apartment, but Ace was hers. They would make this work.

"Hey," he said. "All done?"

She nodded. "Today was an excellent day for Dragonfly Aerial." She hitched her hip on the desk. "Any news on Haye?"

Ace shook his head. "He's in the wind."

"Well, I hope that wind carries him far away from San Francisco." She chewed on her lip. "What does he have to gain from coming after me now? I shared everything I know with the police."

A dark frown settled on Ace's face. "The guy's a murderer, and he's lost everything. I'm not letting that fucker anywhere near my woman."

"Your woman, huh?" She felt warmth in a lot of places.

His sexy smile unfurled. "That's right." He tugged her into his lap. The ancient desk chair squeaked.

"I'm not sure I trust this chair to hold us both."

"I'll keep you safe, *gatinha*." He nibbled on her lips.

"I know you will." She pulled the tie out of his hair and slid her fingers through the silky strands. "The way you stood up to my dad..."

Ace frowned. "He was out of line."

"I guess...a part of me worries that I will fail. He's always taking little digs at me." She sucked in a breath. "And a part of me has worried that I won't be a good mother. I mean, I know nothing about babies."

Ace tipped her face up to his. "You'll be a wonderful, fierce mother. You already are. And I meant what I said to your parents. I know you'll help make me the father this baby needs."

She saw he meant it. Every word. "Thank you," she whispered.

"What your father says doesn't matter, Maggie. He's wrong. You don't have to keep proving yourself to him."

She nibbled her lip and nodded. Ace was right. She'd always gone her own way. She loved her dad, but she'd never let what he said stop her, even when it hurt.

Ace stroked her jaw. "By the way, Gia called. She

told us to meet the gang at ONE65. She wants to celebrate."

Maggie shook her head. "I think Gia just likes any excuse for a party."

Ace laughed. "True. She means well."

"I know. I have to admit that she's a little intimidating. She's so...together. Successful businesswoman, she's gorgeous, and dresses well."

"Well, I think that applies to you, too. You have a successful business, you're gorgeous, and I'll take sexy, painted-on jeans over business suits any day."

Maggie's heart melted. The look on his face said he meant every word. She leaned forward and kissed him.

It was getting hot and heavy when the door opened.

Maggie heard a disgruntled sound and looked up at a scowling Gus.

"Hey, Gus. You finished with Hetty?"

"Yeah."

"Were heading to ONE65 for drinks with friends. To celebrate the asshole being gone." She'd already briefed Gus on Davis Haye and the entire situation.

"The fancy French place," Gus grumbled.

"Yes." She paused. "Want to come?"

She couldn't picture Gus at a fancy bar, but he was a part of her family. Gus, Vander, Ace... They'd all believed in her and supported her when her father hadn't.

"I could drink," Gus said.

She grinned. "I'm not sure coveralls are allowed."

"I'll go home and change. Meet you there."

Maggie touched up her makeup, and swapped her

polo for a slinky, green shirt she kept at the office in case she needed to head into the city after work. She also kept a pair of sexy, knee-high boots with a heel there, too. With a change of earrings to a long, sparkly swing of dangles, she was ready.

When she walked out of the tiny bathroom, Ace looked up and whistled. "*Linda e gostosa.*"

She grinned. *Pretty and hot.* "You're rather hot too, Oliveira."

He nabbed her for a quick kiss.

"Want to ditch this party and head home instead?" he suggested.

"Tempting, but I want to see everybody. And the party is for me."

"Damn."

She nipped his earlobe. "But afterward, I'll rock your world."

He squeezed her ass. "I'll hold you to that."

Ace drove them to ONE65 and valet parked. ONE65 was a six-story, French dining experience. It had everything from a bistro and grill, to a bar and lounge.

They found the others at the bar. Harlow spun, cocktail in hand. "Maggie, where did you get those earrings?"

Soon she was engulfed by the others. Gia, in a slick, blue pantsuit, lifted her drink toward Maggie. Haven was in a suit with a tight skirt. Sofie wore tailored pants and a blouse. It was clear they'd all come from work.

They welcomed her so easily. Soon, she had a nonalcoholic cocktail in hand.

"Here." Gia slipped something over Maggie's head.

She fingered the silky fabric. It was a sash that read "Mommy-to-Be." She laughed. "Thanks."

"How are things with Ace?" Harlow asked.

"Good. He's coming around to the idea of father-hood." She fiddled with her earring. "He stood up to my dad."

"Good. He gets brownie points from me." Gia sniffed. "I'd take Saxon's awful parents down, if I could."

"Mine aren't bad. They're just... Let's say my father has strong views on how I should live my life." She pressed a hand to her stomach. "I'm going to love and support my little peanut. Whatever they want to be or do is fine with me."

"Is it the size of a peanut?" Gia asked.

"Well, it was an apple seed, last time I checked."

"Bub will have grown a bit by now. Let me look." Haven pulled her phone out. "It's a sweet pea!"

"Jeez," Maggie said. "Sometimes I can't believe it's real."

"It'll be a blueberry next week," Haven mentioned. Then she hummed. "Wonder if they make blueberry martinis here?"

"Oh, yum," Gia agreed.

Sofie leaned in. "I haven't tried a blueberry martini before."

"I'm on it," Gia said. "And one with no alcohol for you." She pointed at Maggie.

"Ace is crazy about you," Harlow murmured.

Maggie looked across the room. He was laughing with Saxon. Looking at him made things inside her ache.

In a good way. "I'm part excited, part terrified. He could hurt me, way more than anyone ever has before."

Harlow smiled. "We all get it."

Sofie and Haven nodded.

"I wanted Rhys for ages. I was so afraid he'd shatter me." Haven looked over at her man. "Instead, he's the best thing that ever happened to me."

"Love means taking some risks," Sofie said.

"Yeah," Harlow agreed. "All good things come with risk. You just have to decide how much you want the reward."

Maggie watched Ace turn to Vander. A lot. She wanted it a lot.

Just then, she saw Ace head to the bar. As soon as he'd ordered, a tall, svelte brunette in a black dress with a fall of brown curls sidled up to him. She smiled, tilting her head, and touched Ace's arm.

Oh no, you don't. "I'll be back."

Maggie zeroed in on the bar. The woman stroked Ace's tattooed forearm, her lips moving. He was smiling politely and trying to turn away.

"—and you know a friend of mine. Jenny. She said you rocked her world."

Ugh. Maggie slid up beside Ace and he wrapped a hand around the back of her neck.

"Sorry, the only woman's world he's rocking now is mine," Maggie said.

The brunette's flirty smile flattened. "I heard he doesn't do exclusive."

"He was just waiting for the right one." Maggie

smiled. "He's hot, so I don't blame you for trying." She slid a hand along his abs.

The woman shrugged. "I'm sure he'll be back on the market soon." She winked at Ace. "Find me when you are."

"And I'm sure I can tear those bad extensions out of your hair."

"Maggie—" Ace's warning was laced with amusement.

"Look, tonight, he'll be rocking my world," Maggie said. "And in about eight months, he's going to be rocking our baby to sleep, so don't count on him tracking you down."

The brunette's eyes widened, then she swiveled on her heel and stalked off.

Maggie blew out a breath. "Those extensions look so fake."

He squeezed the back of her neck, his lips brushing her ear. "I like when you get your claws out, *gatinha*."

Looking up at him, she really couldn't blame the woman. He was sexy as hell. "I'm guessing I'm going to need to keep them sharpened."

His gaze turned serious. "I'm only interested in one woman."

Her heart did a little skip in her chest. Then she saw Gus enter the bar, wearing jeans and a polo shirt. She suspected that was as dressed up as he could manage.

"Oh, there's Gus. Avoid any blondes, brunettes, or redheads who are looking to get you naked, Oliveira."

His lips quirked. "I'll do my best."

She headed over to her mechanic.

He scowled, scanning the room. "Fancy."

"Yes."

"This lot are all a bit fancy." He eyed the women.

"Yeah." Maggie nodded at Easton. "That one's a billionaire. And the woman with the strawberry-blonde hair is a princess."

Gus grunted.

"But they're all nice people. Real. And they care. They've all put themselves out to take care of me."

Gus gripped her shoulder. "I'm glad, girlie. You're good people, and you deserve good friends. Your father's always made you feel like shit—"

"Gus—"

"No, I'm not going to badmouth the man. I just want you to know I'm proud of you. And I know you'll be a good mom."

Tears filled her eyes and she sucked them back. "Jeez, Gus, are we having a heart-to-heart?"

"Hell, no. And I'm not buying your rugrat any gifts."

She laughed. "Okay." She lowered her voice. "Thanks, Gus."

Ace appeared. "Gus, can I get you a beer?"

Gus grunted. "You can. I might start to think you're okay after all, Oliveira."

IT WAS A GOOD EVENING. Ace sipped his beer and looked over at Maggie.

She was laughing out loud at a story Haven was telling. He smiled. He liked his friends' women, but now even more so. This was just what Maggie needed. He saw that she was more relaxed than she had been in days.

He smiled to himself. Except when he had her sprawled in his bed, shaking from an orgasm or two.

She threw her head back and laughed again. The sound hit him.

She lived her life to the fullest. She went her own way and did what she loved. She danced in the living room, sang to loud music, flew her helicopter.

All-out.

And she'd love all-out, too. Their child would always be cherished. He felt like he'd been sucker-punched.

"I'm in love with Maggie." He blurted the words out.

His friends all looked at him.

Rome snorted. "You're only just working this out now?"

"Look at Rome, all smug," Saxon said. "It took you a while to admit you were gone for your princess."

They all swiveled to look at Saxon.

Saxon sipped his drink. "Yes, it took me a while, too."

"*Years*," Rhys said.

"I've got her now." He shot a look at Gia and smiled.

She spotted him and blew him a kiss.

"Any PDA tonight and I'll shoot you," Vander warned.

Easton slapped Ace's back. "Maggie's great. You guys are going to make a great family."

Family. Crap, that still made him jittery.

When he looked at Maggie next, she was scanning the room, frowning. Her mommy-to-be sash was still in place.

Ace set his drink down and headed over to her. "*Gatinha*?"

"Ace, have you seen Gus?"

Frowning, Ace looked around. "Not for a while.

"He went to get another beer, and never came back."

Ace's muscles tightened. "I'll look for him. Don't worry. Maybe he's flirting with some woman."

"Gus?" she said skeptically.

"Okay, maybe not."

Ace checked the restrooms, then headed back to the guys.

"Vander," he said quietly. "Maggie's employee, Gus, is missing."

Vander straightened. "When did anyone last see him?"

"He went to get a drink and never returned."

"I'll talk to the bartender." Saxon strode away.

"Could he have gotten a call? Or left?" Vander asked.

"Maybe."

"I'll check outside," Rhys said.

After a quick search, they came back together.

"He got a drink," Saxon said. "Was talking with a guy at the bar, but the bartender didn't notice anything after that."

"Fuck." Ace could see Maggie was worried.

He waved her over. "We can't find him."

"God." She pressed her palms to her cheeks.

Ace helped her sit down. Smelling trouble, the other women came over.

"Stay calm, *gatinha*. I'll check the CCTV. We'll find him."

She nodded.

He left her with the women, then pulled out his phone. He would've preferred his laptop or tablet, but he'd make do. He tapped and opened a program

"Ace?" Vander said.

"I'm tapping into the bar's CCTV."

"You mean hacking."

"It'll be faster than asking." A few more taps. "I'm in."

Ace found the footage for the bar and scrolled back.

"*There*." He saw Gus leaning against the bar. Then a man appeared and started talking to the mechanic.

"The guy's keeping his back to the camera," Vander noted.

Asshole, turn around. Ace ground his teeth together.

"Wait," Rhys said. "Go back and slow it down."

Ace did. And saw what Rhys had spotted.

"Shit." The man had tipped something into Gus' drink.

The older man sipped. After some more talking, Ace noted the way Gus relaxed, and leaned more heavily on the bar.

Then the man took Gus' arm and led him out. The guy didn't look at the camera once.

Shit.

Ace tapped. "Let me see if I can find a camera on the street." He pulled one up. "Got them. Look up, asshole."

Gus was staggering now. Then the man with him turned his head.

Ace sucked in a breath. Vander cursed.

It was Davis Haye.

"Fuck." Maggie would be devastated. If something happened to Gus, she'd never forgive herself. "I'll tell Maggie." Ace scraped a hand through his hair.

A muscle ticked in Vander's jaw. "Ace, take care of her. The rest of us will get the women home, and we'll meet at the office. Tell Maggie we'll find Gus."

Ace nodded.

"I'll call Hunt," Vander said. "And I'll tap my informants on the street. Someone will spot them."

"I'll run any properties Haye might still own or have access to," Ace said.

"Good idea. Send us any good options and we'll check them out."

The other men nodded. Ace took a breath and headed over to Maggie.

She rose, looking pissed, but her hands twisted together nervously. "Did he leave early?" She studied Ace's face and her cheeks paled. "Tell me."

"Haye was here. He struck up a conversation with Gus and slipped something into his drink."

"*No*," she breathed.

Gia patted her back. "Ace and the guys will find him. You can't get too stressed. It's not good for you or the baby."

"Why?" Maggie said. "Why take Gus?"

"Revenge? Because Davis Haye is fucked up? He can't get to you, so he targeted who he could."

"Oh, God." She pressed a hand to her stomach.

"Vander and the guys are going to search for Gus. I'm going to get you home." He pulled her close.

She clutched his shirt. "So, I can sit and do nothing?

Just wait and hope?" She shook her head. "I can't do that, Ace."

"I'm going to run some searches. Find out if Haye has any properties or hidey holes. You can help me."

Her shoulders sagged and he wrapped his arms around her. When she leaned in, and pressed her face against his chest, he held her tight.

He felt a surge of emotion. Every time she turned to him, leaned on him.

She jerked, suddenly tense. "Ace, my parents? If he's targeting people close to me—"

Ace cursed. "I'll contact them and see where they are. I'll get someone on them."

"This is a nightmare."

"Let's go home, *gatinha*. I need to get you safe."

CHAPTER SIXTEEN

M aggie scanned the computer screen again, then watched everything turn into a blur.

She and Ace had been combing property records and picking Haye's life apart.

The guy had so much debt. His properties were all in foreclosure.

She wouldn't feel sorry for the asshole—he was a murderer—but seeing the bankruptcies, the failed marriage, the desperate attempts to regain his wealth, she could practically smell his desperation.

She rubbed her eyes and tried not to fall asleep in the chair.

Beside her, Ace was a machine. He worked much faster than her, and didn't seem to get tired. She could totally picture him as part of some covert government team of badass hackers.

He'd called her parents and assured her that they were safe. She rubbed the back of her neck. He'd organized a man called Ben Ryan, a Norcross contractor, to watch over them.

"Maggie?"

She jerked. "I'm awake."

"Barely." Ace cupped her cheek, his fingers caressing her skin. "You need to rest."

Instantly she thought of Gus. Her throat closed up. "How can I sleep? I'll keep thinking about Gus, about what Haye might be doing to him."

"Hey." Ace pulled her chair close to his. "Gus is tougher than old leather. If anyone can get through this, it'll be him. Vander will find him."

One of the computers pinged.

She tensed. "What is it?"

Ace swiveled and tapped the keyboard. "A few possible properties came up on the search."

Her pulse rabbited. Maybe one of them was where Gus was being held?

"Two look most promising. There's an old warehouse in Bayview. It's in foreclosure, but tied up in litigation. It's empty."

"And the other one?"

"It's in his estranged wife's name, but it doesn't look like she has any ties to it. It's an old apartment building scheduled for demolition soon."

"He put it in her name to hide it."

"Most likely." Ace tapped his phone.

Vander's voice filled the room. "What have you got, Ace?"

"Two properties for you to check. A warehouse in

Bayview. An apartment blocked up for demolition in the Western Addition. Texting the addresses to you now."

"Okay, we'll check them out. We've been running down some leads. A biker contact came through."

"All right. Let us know when you've checked the properties."

"Got it," Vander replied. "Tell Maggie not to worry." Then he was gone.

She sank back in the chair. "Yeah, right. Like I can just turn it off."

"You should get some sleep. It's after midnight."

She swallowed, her throat painfully tight. "After they've searched the properties."

Eventually her nerves drove her to pace. She knew she was running on fumes. Tiredness and worry were dragging on her.

"*Gatinha.*" Ace tugged her onto his lap. He tucked her head under his chin. "Just close your eyes for a minute. Let me hold you."

"I feel safe right here," she whispered.

His arms convulsed on her. She idly traced the tattoos on his forearm.

"I was afraid to trust you. To trust myself."

She felt him kiss the top of her head.

"Don't break my heart, Ace." She couldn't keep her eyes open.

"If I did, I'd break mine too," he murmured.

Maggie figured she dreamed the words, as sleep took her under.

WHEN SHE WOKE, she blinked. Sunlight poked at her eyes. She was on the couch in Ace's office, a soft blanket resting on her.

The sneaky man had lulled her to sleep.

She sat up, and nausea hit instantly. She pressed a hand to her belly. There was no sign of Ace, but the screens were on, and there was a mug with steam coming off it resting beside his keyboard.

Then she heard the murmur of his voice from the living room. It sounded like he was on the phone.

She hurried out. Was there news on Gus? Surely Ace would've woken her up if there was.

His head jerked up. "Morning, *gatinha*." He slid his cell phone away.

"Gus?"

Ace shook his head. "Vander and the guys checked the two properties. Both empty."

Damn. Her arms fell by her sides.

"No news is good news," Ace said.

She looked into his face. "You haven't slept."

"I wanted to keep searching, and I'm used to it. Plus, I'm not pregnant."

"Thank you," she whispered. "For searching."

He kissed her.

"No!" She slammed her hands to his chest. "I need to brush my teeth." And she knew her hair was sticking up everywhere.

"I don't care," he said.

He laid a heavy kiss on her until she pulled away, giggling.

"You might want to get dressed, because your parents are on their way over. That was your dad on the phone."

She froze.

"Your father called. They want to talk to you."

"And you're letting them come?" she asked.

Ace arched a brow. "I expressed to your father that he'd better not say anything that upsets you."

Her chest loosened. "I'll get dressed. If there's anything on Gus, let me know."

After her shower, when Maggie came out, Ace was looking at his phone.

"Your parents are here," he said.

She sucked in a breath. She just needed to be an adult. She was going to be a mother. Her parents, especially her dad, were who they were. They weren't going to change. She had to accept that and not let it affect her.

Her parents crested the stairs and stepped into Ace's living room.

"I love your home, Ace," Maggie's mom said.

"Thank you, Mrs. Lopez."

Her mom's smile was a little overbright. "Please, it's Kiki. We're family now."

Ace inclined his head. "Kiki."

Maggie's father's face was expressionless, but she could tell he looked a little uncomfortable. His gaze fell on her and he paused.

Then her mom raced forward. "Maggie."

Maggie hugged her mom. She was wearing her favorite Chanel Number Five and the comforting scent surrounded Maggie, and thankfully didn't set off her stomach.

"You look good," her mom said "No morning sickness today?"

"I'm feeling a little queasy."

"Ginger worked for me when I was expecting you." Her mom's eyes filled with tears.

"Mom, don't cry."

"My baby is having a baby." She laughed her pretty laugh and squeezed Maggie's fingers. "I'm so excited for you."

"Thanks, Mom."

"Your father is, too." Kiki got a steely look in her blue eyes.

Maggie blinked. Her mother rarely stood up to, or argued with, Maggie's dad.

Her father cleared his throat. "I know I'm not...the easiest man."

Behind her father, a look crossed Ace's face before he hid it.

"Magdalena, I...I love you." His tone was gruff. "Since the moment your mother handed you to me, squalling. Already making yourself known, and doing things your way." Her father smiled. "I was so damn proud. I couldn't believe something so incredible had come from me."

Maggie's heart warmed. "Dad—"

He held a hand up. "Let me finish. I just never think anything, or anyone, is good enough for you, Maggie. I worry about you, and I always will. I know I blunder and show it in a bad way. But I am proud of you, and I do love you." Ruddy color filled his cheeks. He wasn't a man to discuss his feelings.

Maggie went to him and hugged him.

"You'll be a great mama," he said. "And I'll try hard to be a good grandfather."

"Thanks, Dad." Her voice was thick with tears. She lifted her head and met Ace's gaze.

He smiled.

"Sweetie, Ace mentioned your mechanic is missing," her mother said.

Maggie sniffed, worry curdling in her belly. She nodded. "The man who's after me took him."

"Jesus," her father said. "What are the police doing?"

"They have officers searching," Ace said. "And Vander and his team are on the case as well."

"Why don't I make some tea?" Maggie's mom smiled at Ace. "Can I invade your lovely kitchen?"

Ace waved a hand. "It's all yours." A second later, his cell phone rang. "It's Vander." Ace stiffened and pressed the phone to his ear. "Vander? What? Hang on." Ace sprinted for his office.

Heart pounding, Maggie followed, her parents behind her.

"It's on the police scanner—" Ace touched the keyboard.

A bunch of voices came from the speakers, all talking fast.

Ace frowned. "There were shots fired at the airport. At a private hangar." He cursed. "I saw something about a hangar in the name of Bentley Haye. I dismissed it." He cursed and tapped the screen. "Bentley Haye is Davis Haye's son. He's four."

There was more rapid-fire talking from the police audio feed.

"What's happening?" Maggie gripped Ace's arm.

"Police are on the way. Wait!" Ace blinked. "Holy hell." He started laughing.

"What?"

"It sounds like someone set a private aircraft hangar on fire, then escaped...in an old helicopter. He's flying toward the city."

Maggie sucked in a breath. "Gus."

Ace nodded. "Gus."

ACE PULLED his Porsche to a screeching halt at Maggie's landing pad.

An ancient Huey was just setting down to land. A police helicopter was escorting it, hovering in the air above it.

"Oh, my God. An old Huey." Maggie stared at the helo. "What a piece of junk."

The Huey—real name a Bell UH-1 Iroquois—was Vietnam War era. It had patches of rust, and a front panel missing.

Two police cars arrived just after them.

As they started across the landing pad, Gus leaped out of the helicopter.

Maggie made a sound and ran toward him.

Keeping his gaze on her, Ace joined Hunt.

"When Norcross is involved, there's always drama,"

the detective said. "I've got air traffic control up in arms over an unauthorized flight from the airport."

"I'll buy you a drink," Ace said.

"I'll need more than one," Hunt grumbled.

They watched Maggie hug Gus. The man patted her back awkwardly. Ace and Hunt walked over to join them.

"If you cry, girlie, I'm leaving," Gus growled.

Maggie sucked in a noisy breath. "I'm pregnant. It's the hormones."

"I don't care. I don't do tears."

"I'm just glad you're okay."

"No thanks to that asshole, Haye."

Ace noted bruising coming up around Gus's left eye. His wrists were also bruised and raw. He must've slipped some restraints.

There was a roar of a motorcycle engine, and Vander rode in. He parked his BMW bike by Maggie's office, his gaze taking everything in with a glance.

"Let's talk inside," Hunt said.

They settled in the office. Maggie hovered by Gus, who kept shooting her wary glances.

"I'm fine," he gritted out.

"I know, but I was worried. *Really* worried. It's going to take me a while to settle down."

Ace squeezed the back of her neck.

"Oliveira, control your woman," Gus said.

"All right, Gus," Hunt said. "Start at the beginning."

Gus sniffed. "Well, I was at that fancy bar." He recounted what they already knew. "I woke up tied to a chair in an aircraft hangar. That beauty—" he nodded out the window at the old, rusted helicopter "—was in the corner, with some of its engine in pieces. Someone had been trying to fix it." He ran his tongue over his teeth. "Clearly that person was a blind monkey. They had no idea what they were doing."

Hunt just stared for a beat, then shook his head. "Okay, then what?"

"Haye was ranting. He was sweating a lot, too. The guy's lost it. He was screeching that everything is Maggie's fault and he needs to make her pay."

Maggie gasped. "My fault he's a murdering coward who can't run a business? Yeah, right."

"He's unhinged," Gus said. "One wrench shy of a toolbox. He was ranting about revenge, then he calmed down. He talked about getting out of Dodge. Running to Mexico."

Her heart lurched. "Do you think he's gone?"

"Was the last thing he said," Gus said.

"We'll check." Ace hoped the guy was long gone.

"He left the hangar, so I got free of my cuffs. Then I peeked outside. He'd left two of his guards, so I decided the Huey was my best bet. I found some tools, pieced her engine back together, then I set a fire, and flew that baby right out of there." He broke into a deep laugh. "Pretty sure those guards pissed themselves."

"We found them making a run for it," Hunt said. "We have them in custody."

"So it's over." A smile bloomed on Maggie's face.

"We'll see." Ace tugged her close. He wouldn't be smiling until he saw proof that Davis Haye was dead, or in jail.

"Gus, it looks like Haye got a few licks in," Vander

said. "You need to get checked out."

Maggie made a sound and Gus glared at her. "You hug or kiss me again, and I won't be happy." He looked over at Vander. "I don't do hospitals."

"We have a good medic. Hunt's brother."

Gus grunted and Ace guessed it was agreement.

Ace let Maggie hover over Gus while they waited on Ryder.

"You think Haye's gone, and is sunning himself in Cancun?" Ace asked Vander quietly.

Vander sniffed. "I'm not the trusting sort."

Ace nodded. He wasn't either. Especially not when it came to Maggie and their baby.

He headed to her desk and worked on her computer.

"Ace?"

He looked up to find her standing beside him.

"Haye bought a plane ticket to Mexico," he told her.

Her eyes widened and he saw hope flare in them.

"It left an hour ago. It says he was on it."

She blew out a breath. "Thank God."

"Yeah." Ace pulled her down for a kiss.

Once Ryder arrived, he checked Gus over and put some ointment on the man's wrists and gave him the all-clear. Hunt offered to drop Gus home.

Ace saw Maggie yawn—a jaw-cracking one. She'd had a rough night, and not much sleep.

"Naptime," he said.

She shot him a sleepy smile. "I won't say no." She lowered her voice. "Especially if you're with me."

That tone arrowed right to his cock. "Whatever my *gatinha* wants."

Her slow smile warned him that she wanted a lot.

"Ace, Maggie?" Hunt called out.

They looked over at the detective.

"One of my detectives questioned the guards from the hangar. They said Haye told them he was getting on a plane to Mexico."

"He's really gone." Maggie's smile was wide.

Ace wasn't ready to let her out of his sight. "Let's go."

He drove them back to his house and when she moved to skip up the stairs, he grabbed her arm.

"Take it easy on the stairs. I don't want you falling down."

She looked punch-drunk from tiredness. "Okay."

He kept a hold on her hand as they walked upstairs.

"So, I can go back to work as normal tomorrow," she said.

Ace scowled. "Once I confirm it was actually Haye who got on that plane."

"You going to hack airport security?"

He grinned. "I am a hacker, remember."

She shook her head.

He dropped a kiss to the top of her head. "Go and lie down. I'll join you soon."

She shot him a saucy smile and disappeared down the hall.

In his office, Ace dropped into the chair behind his monitors. His fingers danced across the keyboard. It took him a few minutes to hack into the San Francisco Airport security system.

He pulled up the camera at the gate for the flight to Cancun.

It gave him a perfect shot of Davis Haye looking over his shoulder, about to board the plane. It was definitely him.

The air whistled out of Ace, and he sat back.

Haye was gone. It was over.

Ace set up a few little things to keep an eye out for the man. His facial-recognition program would scan for Haye in San Francisco. Just in case.

Ace smiled, some of the weight lifting. Time to celebrate with his woman.

He expected to find her asleep. He didn't expect to find her sprawled on his bed in a tiny scrap of bronze lace.

He sucked in a breath, his skin tightening.

She smiled. "The girls didn't just have baby onesies in all those bags. There was something for me, as well."

She shifted those long legs. She was like a punch to his gut, stealing his breath. "I think it might be for my benefit, too."

Her body showed no signs of the pregnancy yet, but he knew it would come. And he was excited to see those changes.

"You like?" she asked.

"I like what it's covering most of all." He stalked toward her.

Her gaze fell on the bulge in his jeans. "So I see."

He covered her with his body, and cupped one firm breast. "Now, I'm going to fuck your brains out so you're tired enough to nap."

"Oh, if you have to," she said.

As he kissed her neck, he savored her laugh.

CHAPTER SEVENTEEN

Maggie loved driving Ace's Porsche. Her hands flexed on the steering wheel as she drove to her office. It was a bright, sunny Monday morning.

Yesterday, Ace had taken her into work for the morning. Despite telling him to have a day off, Gus had turned up for her scheduled flights.

She'd spent Sunday afternoon watching Marvel movies with Ace, and necking on his couch. It had been pure bliss.

Now, she was off for her first normal day at work—no bad guys, no killer drones, no bodyguards. She'd dropped him at the Norcross office after he'd insisted that she take his sweet red 911.

He'd also made her promise to call him when she got there. And check in every hour.

She smiled, bopping along to the music on the radio that she had turned up way too loud. He was overprotective and she didn't mind.

She patted her belly. "Sweet pea, I hope you're a boy, or your dating life is going to be seriously impeded."

Haye was gone.

She felt like someone had ripped a heavy blanket off her and set her free. She knew she still had to sort out her life, and that made her stomach a little restless. She needed to go back to her apartment now that she was safe. She didn't want to overstay her welcome with Ace.

The phone rang. *Ace*. She thumbed a button for the hands-free.

"Ace, I'm not even there yet."

"I know. I missed you."

Aww. Ace Oliveira could be sweet on top of sexy.

"I'll cook dinner tonight," she said.

"Nice," he said. "Need me to pick anything up?"

Her heart did a flip-flop. All so domestic. "No. I'll grab it." She nibbled her lip. It was best to face things head on. "And we need to talk tonight. About when I should move back to my apartment."

A deep growl cut across the line and her hands tightened on the wheel.

"No," he said.

Maggie blinked. "No what?"

"We're not talking about this now." He sounded pissed. "Call me when you get to work."

He hung up.

She gasped and shook her head. She was the pregnant one who was supposed to be moody, not him.

She finally reached the landing pad. She saw Hetty out, and beside her was the beaten-up Huey. She saw an overall-clad Gus working on the old helicopter.

She locked Ace's car and strode over. "Morning, Gus."

He lifted his chin. He had some bruising around one eye, but otherwise looked his usual self. "No guard dogs today?"

"No. I'm a free woman. Haye is being an asshole somewhere in Mexico."

Gus grunted. "Good riddance."

Maggie eyed the ancient helicopter dubiously. "Didn't the police want to impound this?"

"No. Finders keepers."

"Gus, you can't just steal a helicopter and keep it." She wished.

"I stole it from a criminal. It isn't worth anything. It's mine now."

Shaking her head, she headed for the office.

"Oh, a last-minute job came in," Gus called out.

She cocked her head.

"Husband and wife. She booked a morning tour to celebrate their anniversary."

"Roger that."

"Hetty is ready when you are."

"Thanks, Gus." She paused. "I'm glad you're okay."

He pointed a wrench at her. "No hugging. No kissing. No crying."

With a grin, she saluted him. Once she was inside, she pulled out her phone and called Ace. "I'm here all in one piece."

"Good. Stay out of trouble."

He sounded fine now.

"I always do," she said. "But sometimes it finds me."

"Let's have a drama-free day, *gatinha*."

"You're okay?" she asked carefully. "About talking tonight?"

He made a frustrated sound. "We'll talk tonight."

"Okay, Ace. Bye."

After she hung up, she checked her emails, and also posted on social media. She checked her download stats on the stock sites.

She saw Gus' notation for a woman named Belinda Stanton. Nice of the woman to surprise her husband.

Maggie's chest hitched. Would she and Ace celebrate anniversaries? What if things didn't work out and he ended up marrying someone else?

Ugh. She swallowed the rock in her throat, then took some deep breaths, fighting off the need to be sick.

Shaking her head, she lost herself in her work. Gus wandered in once for coffee, but headed straight back out. The man was obsessed with the Huey.

There was a knock at the door and Maggie looked up to see a forty-something blonde woman bustle in.

"Hi, are you Maggie?" the woman asked.

"I am. And you're Belinda?"

The blonde nodded, clasping her hands together. "I'm *so* excited for the tour. My husband's parking the car. He can't wait."

"That's great. We'll do a quick safety briefing, then head out to the helicopter."

The woman clapped her hands. "Great."

"Would you like something to drink?"

"No, I'm too excited."

Maggie smiled. "When your husband gets here, we'll get started."

"I'm here," a male voice said.

Maggie's mouth went dry. Davis Haye stood in the doorway, a ball cap pulled low over his eyes.

The blonde woman's smile widened. "He's not actually my husband. Yet. He accidentally married the wrong sister." She wrapped herself around the man and the pair kissed.

Oh, ew. Maggie kept her face blank, her pulse racing out of control. "You're not in Mexico."

"No." Haye smiled at her. "I love when people follow my breadcrumbs exactly where I want them to go. Fucking Norcross and that boyfriend of yours had you guarded like the gold at Fort Knox."

"Why come after me? What does it achieve?"

"You ruined *everything*," he roared.

Maggie forced herself not to react. "You're a murderer who took the easy way out."

"I. Lost. Everything." He stalked toward her.

She backed up and bumped into her desk.

God. Terror left her shaky. *Her baby. Ace.* She wouldn't let this asshole destroy her life.

"You're to blame for your own bad decisions," she said.

He leaned in close, invading her space. "If you hadn't put that fucking drone up, and if you'd just kept your mouth shut," he hissed, "everything would've been fine. I had a new building inspector in my pocket. I just needed Marks out of the way, with no link to me."

"You're a murderer." Maggie looked at the blonde.

"You're sleeping with a killer. And he'll kill you when you've outlived your purpose."

Belinda tossed her hair back. "He loves me."

Maggie snorted. "I suspect he told that to your sister, too."

The woman stepped forward and slapped Maggie's cheek. The blow whipped her head to the side.

Belinda's face twisted. "Don't mention that bitch."

"Enough." Haye pulled a compact handgun out of his pocket. "Now, we're heading out to your helicopter. You'll be smiling, like everything is great. You warn the old man out there, who burned down my hangar and stole my helicopter, and I'll fill him full of bullets."

"To be fair, your helicopter is a piece of junk," Maggie said.

Haye waved the gun and her breath stuck in her throat.

"Out to the helicopter. Now. Be convincing." He slipped on a pair of reflective sunglasses. With the hat and glasses, he just looked like any other guy.

Crap. Crap. Crap.

Maggie desperately tried to think of a way to stall Haye and slow him down.

How could she alert Gus without giving it away? She felt the gun barrel jammed into her back.

"Remember, warn him and I'll shoot him." Haye's voice was stone cold. It shot ice through her veins.

She didn't doubt him for a second.

Maggie pulled in a shuddering breath and led the couple outside.

"Smile," Haye murmured. "Like you're selling us the

tour."

Maggie waved an arm. "That's the Golden Gate Bridge over there. I'd like to drop you off it."

"Keep moving."

Gus looked over and Maggie managed a cheerful wave. Her mechanic looked at her, then the couple, then nodded.

"We're going to get in your sexy bird, and we're going to take off," Haye said.

She swallowed. "Then what?"

"You'll take us for a nice little tour of the Bay," he said. "Then we'll find a quiet place to shoot you and push you out. Belinda, here, can fly."

The woman's eyes gleamed. "I took lessons."

As Maggie stared into Haye's face, she saw he wasn't quite all there. He'd lost rational thought somewhere along the way.

Damn. He was a man on a mission. He couldn't be reasoned with.

No. She kept her face carefully blank, while her insides were alive. She *wasn't* giving up. She had too damn much to live for.

A tiny spark of life was depending on her. Hers and Ace's child deserved to live.

Maggie climbed into Hetty. She just had to wait for the right opportunity.

***

ACE TRIED to shake off his bad mood and focus on the screens in front of him.

He had a small backlog of work to get done, but damn if he didn't miss having Maggie with him.

A part of him wasn't ready for her to be out of his sight. He hadn't told her, but he had a tracker on his car, and he'd set up a facial-recognition alert for Haye.

If the guy showed on any CCTV within a certain radius of Maggie's business, it would trigger an alarm.

The thought of her moving out of his place curdled his gut.

Fuck, no.

Maggie was *his*. They had a baby on the way. He was in love with her.

Tonight, he'd make that very clear. Tonight, he'd tell her that they were getting married.

An alarm pinged on his computer and his muscles locked.

He touched the screen and an image filled it.

Davis Fucking Haye.

On the street outside Dragonfly Aerial.

"*No.*" Ace rang Maggie's cell phone as he sprinted for the door.

No one answered.

The Norcross office was pretty quiet today, with most of the guys out in the field. He saw Vander step out of the kitchen holding a coffee mug. One look at Ace's face and Vander snapped to attention. "What's wrong?"

"Haye just showed up on CCTV at Maggie's office. She's not answering her phone."

Vander cursed and set his coffee mug down. "Let's move."

Once again, they sprinted to the SUVs.

"Anyone else around?" Ace asked.

"Rhys is out. Rome's escorting Sofie to an event in LA. Saxon is following up on some leads on the Courtland job."

Fuck. As Vander tore out of the warehouse, Ace tried to find some calm.

Be okay, Maggie. Hold on.

"I can't lose her."

"You won't." Vander broke the speed limit as they roared north.

"Gus should be there." Ace quickly pulled out his tablet and did a quick search. Once he had Gus' cell phone number, he punched it in.

Vander honked the horn, and yanked the wheel. They dodged around a slow-moving car and picked up speed.

"What?" Gus' grumpy voice.

"Gus, it's Ace. I picked up Haye on CCTV near you guys."

Gus' curse was creative, and anatomically impossible.

"Have you seen him?" Ace asked.

"No. Maggie's got a couple here for a tour. They're celebrating their anniversary."

"Could the guy be Haye?"

"Dunno. Maybe. Only saw him from a distance, and he was wearing a hat and glasses. I didn't get a close look."

Damn. "Maggie isn't answering her phone."

"She won't when she's with clients."

Ace blew out a breath. "Keep an eye out for Haye, but don't intervene, Gus. He's dangerous."

"I know, Oliveira. You on your way?"

"Yes."

"With your badass boss?"

"Yes."

"See you soon."

Ace relayed the details to Vander.

"We'll be there in five minutes," Vander said.

Those five minutes felt like five years.

As Vander screeched to a halt, Ace saw Maggie walking with a couple across the landing pad to Hetty.

The guy was standing too close to her. Right behind her. He had a cap pulled low over his face, but the clothes were the same as what Haye was wearing in the CCTV image.

"It's Haye," Ace snapped.

"He's got a weapon on her," Vander said.

They slid out of the X6.

The trio were near the helo now.

They got inside and the rotors started to move.

No! "Vander, we need a plan." One that didn't get Ace's woman killed.

Vander opened the trunk of the X6. A heavy-duty lockbox was bolted in the back. Vander quickly unlocked it using his palm print.

It was filled with weapons and he handed a Glock to Ace before taking an M4 assault rifle for himself.

"Let's move before they take off," Vander said.

Weapons up, they moved across the landing pad.

The wind from the rotors buffeted them.

Ace came up on Haye's side, his Glock up.

When the man spotted him through the glass of the

cockpit, he lifted his own weapon, but held it aimed at Maggie's head.

Fuck. Ace's jaw worked.

Maggie's face was pale, but he saw that she was pissed.

Vander stepped up on the other side, the rifle up. He knew exactly how to use it.

Haye leaned over and rammed the barrel of the gun against Maggie's temple. She winced.

Ace couldn't breathe. He wanted to pound the man to mush.

Haye's lips moved.

Maggie's mouth firmed into a flat line, and she met Ace's gaze.

Shit, he just wanted to reach in there and pull her out.

A second later, the helo's skids lifted off the concrete.

No. *No.* His heart was beating so hard he couldn't breathe.

He wouldn't let her face this alone. Wouldn't let this asshole end all that was Maggie.

Ace jammed the Glock in the back of his waistband.

As the helo lifted off, he ran after it, sprinting toward the end of the pier.

"Ace!" Vander roared.

But all his focus was on Maggie.

The helicopter lifted higher and Ace leaped off the end of the pier, out over the water...

And grabbed onto one of the skids.

He gripped hard as the helicopter soared up into the sky and out over San Francisco Bay.

CHAPTER EIGHTEEN

Fear tasted bad.

Maggie felt so horribly alone. She knew that Ace was back there, afraid and angry.

She kept her hands as steady as she could on the controls. The water was blue below, and off to her left was Alcatraz.

She turned down the calls from air traffic control.

"That's it, Ms. Lopez," Haye drawled.

In the backseat, Belinda smiled smugly. "This is a sexy helicopter." She stroked the leather seats. "Once we get rid of her, and get away, baby, I want to fuck you in the back."

What the hell was wrong with these people?

"I'm pregnant," Maggie said.

She saw Haye frown, then he raised his gun again. "Keep flying, and shut up."

"Yeah, we don't care if you're knocked up," the woman said.

Maggie looked sideways at Haye. There was a slim

chance she could talk them out of this. He was unhinged, but for her baby, she had to try.

"But Davis here is a father. He has babies with your sister."

"Shut up about my sister!"

"Killing me won't change anything. You should've got on that plane to Mexico."

"It'll make me feel better to kill you," he bit out. "If not for you, I'd be in my office, my building project would be progressing, and—"

"Your marriage wouldn't have fallen apart?" Maggie said.

"He hates that bitch I'm related to." Belinda leaned forward. "He loves *me*. Tell her, baby."

But Haye was silent, looking straight ahead out the cockpit window.

"I'm thinking you're just revenge," Maggie told the woman.

It seemed revenge was a bit of a thing for Davis Haye. Screwing his wife's sister. Killing the building inspector. Coming after Maggie.

Belinda leaned between the seats. "Quiet, bitch." She slapped at Maggie.

Maggie jerked the controls and the helicopter wobbled. She struggled to right it.

"Belinda!" Haye snapped. "Get back in your seat."

With a sniff, the woman sat back.

"You made your choices, Haye," Maggie said. "You murdered a man. You cut corners. You fucked up."

"You want to be quiet now." His icy tone made Maggie's mouth dry.

"You've lost your grip on reality. I just happened, unluckily, to end up in your path."

"Soon you'll be dead, so you won't need to worry."

Screw that. Maggie's hands clenched on the controls.

She glanced up and saw the small, silver chain dangling off the controls. It was her pretty dragonfly pendant from Ace. From the man who'd meant something to her right from the moment she first met him.

A man she knew would find a way to come for her.

A man who'd never let her down.

Suddenly, she pretended to check the gauges and grabbed the chain, slipping it into her palm. The end of the dragonfly was sharp. It wouldn't do much damage, but it was better than nothing.

She pulled in a steadying breath, then lunged across the seat, swiping at Haye.

She managed to knock the gun out of his hand, and it hit the floor. He cursed, and she rammed the dragonfly into his eye.

His ear-piercing bellow made Maggie grimace.

"Fucking bitch. My eye!" He shoved her back into her seat. There was blood on her hand.

Haye had one palm pressed to one side of his face. Blood oozed between his fingers.

Belinda attacked from the back in a flurry of slaps and hits. Maggie shoved an elbow back, and caught the blonde in the head.

With a cry, Belinda fell back on her ass, dazed.

Maggie saw Haye scrambling to find the gun. She jerked the controls and the helicopter flew sharply to the left. Haye fell back in his seat, his elbow smacking the side window.

Maggie unclipped her belt, then reached over and punched him.

"Fuck," he bit out. He swung out and his knuckles caught her mouth. She tasted blood. Damn, he'd split her lip.

She kept hitting him. She couldn't let him get the gun.

He tried to grab her hair, then shoved her head forward. Her forehead slammed into the controls. Pain exploded behind her eyes, and stars danced in her vision.

"You will die today," he said.

Breathing heavily, Maggie steadied the helicopter. "No, I have too much to fight for, too much to live for."

She jabbed at him again. She hit his cheek and he yelled.

Suddenly, Belinda flew into the front from the back.

"Stop hurting him," the woman screeched.

Dammit, the woman was half in Maggie's lap, pinning Maggie to the seat. Belinda twisted and raged.

Maggie got an elbow to her chin. *Ow*. Belinda's knuckles rammed into Maggie's ribs. But she was more worried about what Haye was doing.

"You're a shame to women everywhere," Maggie said. "We help each other, not hurt each other for the sake of a man."

"Shut up!" Belinda lurched again.

She smacked the side door by Maggie and it flung open.

Oh. *Fuck*.

The wind rushed at them. Belinda's hair flew everywhere, getting in Maggie's eyes. The wind ripped at Maggie's clothes, and her eyes watered.

She was excruciatingly conscious that she didn't have her belt on, and neither did Belinda.

"We'll fall out, you crazy woman," Maggie roared.

Belinda shifted again and bumped the controls. The helicopter dove forward.

Fucking hell. Maggie awkwardly reached around the woman's body. "Hold still." She frantically grabbed the controls, and pulled them out of the dive.

Belinda stopped fighting. Maggie grabbed the door and slammed it closed.

When she looked back, it was to stare straight into the gun aimed at her face.

Her heart did a hard thump-thump against her ribs.

"Now, I want you to climb in the back, Ms. Lopez," Haye said. "Belinda, get in the pilot's seat."

Maggie stared at him, helplessness rising up to choke her.

She had no way out.

Oh, Ace.

Haye jerked the gun. "Now."

Maggie climbed into the back.

Belinda gave her a dirty look, then settled into Maggie's seat.

Maggie's belly was a hard churn of so many emotions. "This won't end here," she said. "My man, my friends at Norcross Security, they will hunt you down. There will be no revenge. You'll be hunted down like a dog."

Haye paused, something moving through his gaze.

Then he straightened and climbed into the back with Maggie.

He pressed the gun to her chest.

"I'm too smart to get caught. I'll be long gone before they get close."

Maggie laughed. "My man, the father of my baby, he's former NSA Red Team. He's a brilliant hacker and can make computers dance to his tune. And Vander..." She smiled. "You'll never see him coming. Ace will find you, and Vander will take you down. That's what my friends do."

Haye's face twisted. Then he reached over and slid open the side door. The rush of air and the beat of rotors filled her ears.

Fear carved out Maggie's insides and she pressed a hand to her belly.

I'm sorry, sweet pea. Sorry I can't give you a chance. I'm sorry, Ace.

Haye gestured to the door.

Oh. *Shit.* Her heartbeat was so loud it drowned out everything else and rivaled the thump of the rotors.

She gripped the edge of the door, and sensed Haye lifting the gun.

Maggie looked down at the water far below...

And jerked in shock. Ace was crouched on the skid, his hair loose and blowing around in the wind.

His face was set like stone. Then he surged up and into the helo.

Maggie threw herself to the side. She heard the gun go off, and Haye curse, followed by the thud of flesh on flesh.

She looked up to see Ace and Haye wrestling inside the helicopter.

———

HIS RAGE WAS icy hot as Ace fought Haye.

The fucker tried to kill Maggie, was trying again.

It ended today. *Right here.*

Ace punched the man in the head.

Haye roared and bucked. They rolled in the tight confines of the helicopter and something jammed into Ace's back.

Haye got a decent hit in, snapping Ace's head back.

"I'll kill you, then her," the man yelled. "She'll die, nice and painfully."

The guy was short a circuit or two. Ace rolled and got on top of the man, and grabbed his shirt. He hammered several blows into Haye's face.

Blood dribbled from the man's mouth, and he swung futilely.

"It ends here, Haye. I won't let you hurt her. She's mine to protect, mine to love."

With a roar, Haye tried to sit up.

Maggie appeared and wrapped a forearm around the man's neck from behind. She yanked him back.

Haye choked.

Ace smiled grimly and punched him hard.

With a groan, Haye sagged. His head dropped forward. He slumped to the floor, out cold.

Ace met Maggie's gaze. He smiled and she smiled back.

"You came." She shook her head. "You jumped onto a *helicopter*. You're crazy."

"About you."

"Davis!" A wild screech from the cockpit.

Suddenly, Haye's bitch dove into the back, kicking and clawing at Ace.

Oh, hell. As the helicopter lurched, Ace tried to grab the woman.

She slammed against him and they spun. They hit the side of the helo.

"Go," he cried at Maggie.

He saw Maggie leap into the pilot's seat. A second later, the helo leveled out. But she kept looking back, watching the fight.

Ace caught the blonde, trying not to hurt her. They rammed into the seats, and teetered to the side.

Too fucking close to the open door.

"Ace, look out!" Maggie yelled.

The blonde got a hard slap in, rocking him back on his feet. He tried to kick her, but she danced out of the way.

Her smile was ugly and mean. She charged Ace, trying to push him out the door.

Ace swiveled to the side at the last second.

The woman over-balanced, and fell out the open door.

He lunged for her. Her scream was high-pitched.

But he was too late.

He gripped the door frame as he watched her fall.

"Fuck," Ace yelled against the wind.

Maggie bit her lip. "I'm trying to feel sorry for her."

Maggie wrinkled her nose. "Nope. Got nothing more than a tiny dribble."

Ace didn't blame her. The woman had made her own selfish choices.

"You okay?" Maggie called out.

"Yes, *gatinha*—"

Suddenly, Haye lunged up off the floor.

Shit.

Ace threw his arms up. Maggie jerked the controls, and the helo tilted. He tried to brace himself to stop from losing his balance.

"Don't move!" Haye had found his gun, and now aimed it at Ace.

Ace froze, watching the man steadily. Then Haye shifted and pressed the barrel into the back of Maggie's skull.

Oh, fuck.

"It's over, Haye," Ace said.

"Not if I'm holding the gun."

"If you kill her, the only helicopter pilot, we all die."

Haye moved and fired. Maggie choked on a scream.

Ace's heart tried to burst out of his chest

The bullet hit the window on the other side of the cockpit. The glass was now a web of cracks.

Haye rammed the barrel back into the back of Maggie's neck and she winced.

"I'm so over you and your drama," Maggie yelled. "Blaming everyone else for your mistakes. Just grow some balls."

"Maggie," Ace warned.

It looked like she was over caring. Over being worried and scared.

"Just man up, Haye!" she yelled.

Ace sensed the man coiling...

Ace launched himself at Haye. There was another gunshot.

They crashed to the floor again, wrestling near the open door.

Maggie turned the helicopter again, tilting them away from the door. Ace leaped up, and Haye rammed a fist into his gut. They gripped each other and staggered.

Maggie leveled the helicopter and Ace kicked Haye's hand. The gun flew out of the door, and Haye launched himself at Ace.

They slammed through the gap in the seats to the cockpit, and hit the controls.

The helicopter jerked wildly. Maggie cursed.

As they struggled, Ace yanked the man into the back. He had a quick glimpse of Maggie gritting her teeth, struggling to get control of the helo back.

"Maggie, you can do it," Ace cried out.

He slammed another punch at Haye, then blocked the man's returning cross.

The helo steadied.

Suddenly, Haye roared and charged Ace like an NFL defender. The man crashed into him, and they flew toward the open door.

"Ace!" Maggie yelled.

At the last second, he gripped the edge, catching himself. But some of his body was outside the helicopter, feet dangling, the wind tearing at him. Haye hammered at Ace's fingers, and kicked him.

"Stop!" Maggie screamed.

But Ace's fingers loosened and he slipped.

Fuck.

He grabbed the bottom edge of the door frame, his legs dangling completely outside.

All of a sudden, there was another *thump-thump-thump*, a sound out of sync with Hetty's rotors.

Ace looked up, and saw Haye lifting his foot to kick Ace in the face.

Then a flash of movement off to the left. An old, battered Huey flew up beside them.

Gus sat in the pilot's seat, while Vander stood in the open side doorway. The wind tugged at his suit pants, white shirt, and his dark hair. He held a rifle in his arms, aimed toward them.

Crack.

Haye made a sound and staggered. Blood bloomed on the man's shirt. He fell backward and crashed into the seats.

Ace quickly pulled himself into the helicopter and yanked the door shut.

"Ace! My God," Maggie yelled.

"I'm okay." He reached out and touched the back of her neck fleetingly, then he crouched over Haye.

He punched the man once, and then again. He followed that with a kick, and another punch.

Haye groaned and Ace flipped him over, yanked out the man's shoelaces, and tied his hands behind his back.

"Is it over?" Maggie's voice was a little shaky.

Ace rose and moved over to her. He pressed a quick kiss to her lips. "It's over."

"Are you all right?"

"I am now. You?"

"Yes."

He ran a hand over her hair. "How about we land this bird?"

She nodded rapidly.

As they aimed toward the San Francisco skyline, the Huey moved in close beside them. Gus saluted, and Vander nodded.

Then both helicopters flew back toward the city.

CHAPTER NINETEEN

As Maggie flew in to land, the flashing emergency lights of a dozen vehicles at her landing pad glittered in her eyes.

It was really over.

The skids touched down, and she released a long, shaky breath.

Ace opened the side door.

Hunter Morgan leaped into the helo.

"Special delivery," Ace said, toeing Haye.

"You guys do everything the hard way." Hunt eyed the man dispassionately, then waved two cops in. They dragged the man out.

"A woman fell into the Bay," Ace told Hunt.

"Shit."

"Belinda," Maggie said. "His sister-in-law."

Hunt nodded. "We'll take care of it." His green eyes swung Maggie's way. "You okay?"

"I wish I could have a stiff drink."

Hunt smiled. "I think you'll be fine." He followed the cops out.

Ace climbed into the seat beside her.

"I don't think my legs will hold me," she told him.

"They don't need to. I'll hold you up."

He pulled her out of her seat and Maggie happily climbed onto his lap. His arms curled so tight around her that it almost hurt.

She didn't care one bit.

"Jeez, Maggie. When I saw that asshole had you..."

"I know." She pressed her face into Ace's neck. "And when you were fighting him..." So many times, they'd gone too close to the open door. Air shuddered out of her. Then she saw the battered old Huey coming in to land.

"Thank God for Gus and Vander," she said.

"Yeah," Ace agreed.

"Is it really over, Ace?"

He tilted her face up. "It's really over. Haye is going away for a very long time."

"Some part of me almost felt sorry for him. That he lost everything." Then her anger spiked. "But instead of smartening up, making better choices, he kept taking shortcuts and making selfish decisions."

Ace toyed with her hair. "Yeah. It made me realize we really are who we make ourselves. We aren't our blood, or what happens to us. We aren't the doubts or things other people think of us." He tugged on her hair. "It's *our* choices and actions that define us. When things get tough, that's who we really are."

"When did you get so wise?" she asked with a smile.

"Since a smart-mouthed, independent pilot blew into my life."

"Haye blamed everyone else for everything in his life."

Ace nodded. "And when you blame others and refuse to take responsibility or control, you've already lost. Being a good dad, that's on me. It doesn't matter who contributed to my DNA. Hell, it wouldn't even matter if my biological father had raised me. It's still all on me. And what happened to Rodrigo, I'll never forgive myself for it completely, but I know his choice played a part, and that I learned from what happened." He cupped her face. "I'm going to be a good father to our baby."

Warmth bloomed in her chest. It swelled, filling her. "I know, Ace. I always knew."

"And it doesn't matter what your father thinks or says, as long as you know in your heart that you're living your life the way you want. The way *you* know is right."

"I am," she whispered.

Ace kissed her.

He tasted like home and sexy promises.

Then he pulled back, and a scowl crossed his face. "And you aren't moving out of my place."

"Ace, I—"

"No. We're going to make a home together. Be a family."

Her breath hitched. "What are you saying?"

"I'm saying that you're mine, Magdalena Lopez." He sucked in a breath. "And I love you. I love your courage, grit, and loyalty. I love your long legs and your saucy laugh. I... just love you. You snuck in and stole my heart, but I want you to keep it. I want you to be mine."

"Does that mean you're mine, too?" Her chest was so tight, tears threatening.

"Yes. Always. If you want me."

She laughed. "God, Ace. I'm crazy in love with you."

The next kiss was rougher, harder, and sexier.

A throat cleared very nearby.

"Can you let the girl up for air, Oliveira?" Gus grumped.

They both looked back. Gus, Vander, Saxon, and Rhys stood outside of the helo.

"We'd like to hug her, too," Vander said.

Smiling, Maggie kissed Ace and climbed out of the helicopter.

Gus' hug was quick, a little awkward, but firm.

"Thanks for coming after me," she said.

Her mechanic grunted. "You're a decent boss. I didn't want to break another one in."

Maggie laughed.

"And you have to take back all the things you said about my Huey. It saved the day."

"It sure did."

Then she found herself in Vander's arms.

"Thanks, Vander."

"I'm glad you're okay. And I'm glad Haye is done." Vander stroked a hand down her arm. "You and Ace okay?"

She shot him a blinding smile. "He loves me."

"He'd be an idiot not to. Glad I don't have to rough him up."

"Incoming," Saxon warned.

The gang arrived.

Gia led the charge. Maggie saw her parents there, as well. Her mom had clearly been crying, as her eyes were red rimmed.

Maggie was hugged and patted, and then checked over by Ryder. Her mom held her tight, and even her dad kept touching her—stroking her back, patting her shoulder.

"Is our grandbaby okay?" her mom asked.

"I think so, although I'm hoping to have a few far-less-stressful months."

Her mom laughed, then kissed Maggie's cheek.

"Mom, Dad, I'm moving in with Ace. I love him." She looked over to meet Ace's gaze. He wasn't far away, talking with Hunt and Vander. "And he loves me."

"The man leaped onto a helicopter to save you." Her father's voice was gruff. "I'd say he's absolutely crazy in love with you."

She smiled. "He's everything I ever wanted. And he'll be an amazing daddy."

Her father gripped her hand. "I'm glad. My baby girl deserves all of that."

Love for both of them hit her. They weren't perfect, but neither was she. Underneath it all, she knew they loved her, and she always needed to remember that.

She hugged her father, then headed over to Ace.

"*Gatinha*." He opened his arms. "You need to get off your feet."

She leaned into him.

"You all right?" he asked.

"Yes," she replied. "Everything's more than all right."

Ace swept her into his arms. "I'm taking my woman home."

As he carried her across the landing pad, everyone called out their goodbyes.

"I love you, Ace."

"I love you too, Maggie."

"I'd fight a hundred bad guys, if it meant I got you in the end."

"*Querida*." He set her feet down by his Porsche. "No more bad guys. Let's have a boring life for a bit."

She pressed her hands to his chest. "Not too boring, I hope." She stroked the skin at the neck of his shirt.

He cocked a brow. "Has the near-death experience left you a little worked up?"

She leaned closer. "Maybe. Maybe I just want to celebrate us being alive."

He slid a hand down and squeezed her ass. "Then let's get home, *gatinha*, and celebrate."

CRAP, he was late.

Ace turned onto his street and saw all the familiar cars parked outside his place. Work had run over.

And now he was late for his own baby shower.

He parked the Porsche in his garage and leaped out. As he raced to the front door, he heard music and laughter inside.

Gia opened the door, wearing a sexy, red wrap dress.

She tapped the toe of her high heel. "You're late, Oliveira."

"I know."

"Luckily, your baby mama is having too much fun to miss you too much."

He kissed Gia's cheek. "Thanks for organizing this. She's been excited."

Gia softened a little. "She deserves that. So do you."

It had been three months since Davis Haye had attacked Maggie. Since then, things had been busy.

Haye was in jail.

Maggie had moved in officially.

They'd had an ultrasound, and he'd seen his baby and heard its little heart beating.

Thankfully, life had been normal—no murder attempts, no kidnappings, no problems.

He'd bought Maggie a nice BMW X3. It fit her drones in the back, and had plenty of room for a baby seat.

Life was good.

He slung an arm across Gia's shoulders as they headed up the stairs.

"How's the wedding planning going?" he asked.

"Extravagantly," she answered.

"Lucky Saxon is loaded. And totally in love with you."

Gia smiled.

The living room was filled with people—friends and family.

He spotted his mom and dad talking with Maggie's mom and dad. Leo Lopez was drinking a frothy blue drink. There were lots of pink and blue drinks with straws all topped with pacifiers.

Cute.

Ace had warmed to Leo. The man did love his daughter, he just didn't always get things right. The prospect of a grandchild had mellowed him a little. He and Kiki had bought so much baby gear, that Maggie had finally lost it.

They were now creating their own nursery for the baby at their house, for future visits.

The Norcross guys and their women were dotted around the big room. Saxon and Rhys were on the couch working on something on the coffee table.

"What are they doing?" Ace asked.

"A game. Make a baby out of Play-Doh. There are prizes for the cutest, the ugliest, the weirdest."

Ace raised a brow.

"The diaper toss game is next." She grinned. "You have to toss a diaper into a trashcan. You'll need the practice."

He laughed. He no longer got that wave of sheer panic at the thought of having a baby. He and Maggie were reading books and checking out websites. He was going to be a dad, and he was going to do it well.

He saw the kitchen island was covered in delicious looking foods. There were cupcakes topped with pictures of little baby bottles, pacifiers, and little baby feet, as well as brigadeiros—classic Brazilian fudge balls covered in chocolate sprinkles. They were no doubt made by his father.

Then he spotted Maggie.

She was in jeans and a pretty green top. She still

didn't look very pregnant, but she now had a sweet curve to her belly and her breasts were a cup size larger. Ace spent a lot of time kissing her belly and talking to the baby.

She turned her head and saw him. Her smile widened. She was in that radiant, glowing phase of pregnancy—where her skin glowed and her hair gleamed.

He waved and she blew a kiss at him.

"Ace."

He turned to find his brother grinning at him, holding a cupcake in each hand.

"Hey there, *maninho*." He hugged Rodrigo. "How are you liking the party?"

"The food is yummy. I love cupcakes."

Rodrigo took a bite, icing smeared on his upper lip. He looked a lot like his dad with a trim build and dark hair. They both had their mother's brown eyes.

Ace smiled. "Have as many of them as you like, but don't get sick."

His brother nodded solemnly. "Maggie said she has a present for me."

"She does. You'll like it." It was a fun T-shirt she'd had printed that said "best uncle ever."

Much to Ace's delight, Rodrigo loved Maggie, and she was great with him. They visited him each week, and he occasionally had a day out with them. He was thrilled about the baby.

"Maggie let me touch her tummy. I think I felt the baby move."

"It's a bit early yet, bro. It needs to get a bit bigger yet." Ace was hoping to feel his child move soon.

"I need more cupcakes," Rodrigo said.

Ace squeezed his brother's arm. "Go."

Next, Ace stopped by the bar. Vander cracked the tops off two beers and held one out to Ace.

"You aren't making Play-Doh babies?" Ace asked.

"Fuck, no," his boss said.

"What about the diaper toss?"

Vander shot him a look.

"Right." Ace sipped his beer. "Jeez, look at this, a baby shower." He spotted Hunt and Ryder talking to some of Maggie's friends, including Gus, who looked totally out of place. Maggie's pilot friend was also there with her wife. Penny was going to take care of flying for Maggie's business while Maggie took time off after the baby arrived.

"I've got a baby coming in a few months," Ace said in wonder.

"Happy?" Vander asked.

He looked at Maggie. "Yeah." She kept him on his toes—making him laugh, getting him angry, loving him.

"Good. Keep her happy, or I'll take you down."

Ace smiled at Vander. "That's not going to be a problem."

They clinked their bottles together.

Ace decided he needed to kiss his woman. He stole her away from some of her friends.

"Hello, *gatinha*."

"Hi, Oliveira."

He nibbled on her lips. "Sorry I was late."

"Vander told me you were finishing up with some work."

He nodded. "How was your day?"

"Great." She smiled and looked around the room. "And the shower is wonderful. There are so many gifts."

He eyed the pile in the corner. A giant teddy bear topped the stack. It was almost as big as he was. "Jeez, who bought the bear."

Maggie grinned. "Gus. He also bought a cute little mechanic shirt and hat."

The old guy was so smitten. Last week, he'd set up a playpen in Maggie's office in preparation for the baby's arrival.

"How's our avocado?" He put a hand on her belly, and felt that subtle curve.

"Awesome."

They weren't going to find out if it was a boy or girl. They were just calling the baby whatever object it was the size of.

Maggie put her hand over his. The princess-cut diamond on her finger twinkled.

He'd proposed a month ago, on the rooftop deck under the stars, and Maggie had said yes. She'd expressed just how happy she was about it afterward, in their bed.

They decided to have the wedding after the baby arrived. They didn't want to have too much to deal with all at once. Maggie was stressed out just thinking about decorating the nursery. Plus, she was adamant that she wanted an awesome dress, with no baby bump.

"I didn't know I could be this happy," Maggie said.

He nuzzled her neck. "This is just the start, *gatinha*. We have so much ahead of us."

"And we'll rock it all. Parenting, marriage, love."

"We're already rocking that last one."

"I do love you, Ace Oliveira. So much it leaves me breathless."

He pressed his lips to hers. "If you can't breathe, I'll do it for you. I'll be staying right by your side, forever."

She smiled. "*Para siempre.*"

"No, it's *para sempre.* I'll get you speaking Portuguese eventually." He kissed his fiancée again.

CHAPTER TWENTY

Vander

Vander had the sudden realization that he'd probably be going to a lot more baby showers in the not-too-distant future.

Fuck. He sipped his beer.

He watched Ace and Maggie kiss. She beamed up at Vander's tech guru. Vander was happy for them. He'd put up with tons of weddings and baby showers if his friends and family were safe and happy.

He knew all too well that life could be fucked. You had to take the good any way you could find it. He found his in crafting his life just how he liked it—his own business, his own place, and he liked nothing more than the solitude of his loft apartment above the office. Watching an ice hockey game with a glass of excellent bourbon.

He'd spent years fighting for his country. So far down in the darkness, fighting dangers most people never knew existed. Around him, he heard the clink of glasses, laughter, happy conversation. Most of these people would never know the things he'd seen, and he was damn happy about that fact.

"Vander."

Ryder Morgan stepped up beside him.

Vander sipped his beer and shook off the dark memories. "Ryder. Please tell me you didn't do the diaper toss."

The paramedic grinned. "Came second. Easton won. Your brother has a hell of an arm."

"Always did. He was pure beauty on the baseball field in high school."

Ryder scanned the room and sipped his own beer. "You heard Camden's getting out and coming home?"

Camden Morgan was the third Morgan brother, who was currently serving overseas on a Ghost Ops team.

"I did."

Ryder turned. "He mentioned you called him. Made him a job offer."

Cam had excellent skills and was cool under fire. Vander looked at Ryder over his beer bottle. "Yeah."

Ryder nodded. "Good. He should've gotten out a year ago. He'll need something once he's back."

Yeah, Vander knew that feeling, too. Getting back, after spending so much time switched "on" and fighting for your life, was hard. He'd spent years giving orders, protecting his team, taking down the bad guys. It had been tough to transition back to civilian life.

And Vander was well aware that he'd never quite fully adjusted.

Cam Morgan probably wouldn't, either. He'd made a solid name for himself in Ghost Ops.

"I'll look out for him, Ryder."

The other man released a breath. "Thanks, Vander." Then he smiled and slapped a hand to Vander's back. "So, when will we be having a baby shower for you?"

Vander shot his friend a look.

Ryder chuckled. "Man, did you expect your brothers and your best friends to go down so easily?" The paramedic shook his head. "Seems when the right one comes along, bam, you're down for the count."

Vander had never been down for the count. In fact, he did everything he could to avoid it.

His gaze drifted over the room. Easton had an arm around a laughing Harlow. Rhys was nuzzling Haven's ear, and saying something that made her blush. And dammit, Saxon was kissing Gia like there was no one else in the room.

When Vander wanted a woman, he found one. He was well-aware he intimidated many, or flat-out scared them, with his intensity. Then there were the few who liked the danger and approached him for it. Those ones he avoided.

But mostly, he disliked anyone in his space, so his hookups weren't frequent.

He liked his space and solitude.

"I'm going to get some food," Ryder said. "Thanks again, Vander. About Cam."

One of Maggie's friends walked past, shooting Vander an inviting smile.

Vander kept his expression blank. Shit, he could no longer point the overeager ones in his brothers' directions anymore. But he noticed Ryder head in the woman's direction, thankfully taking her off his hands.

A tell-tale tingle ran across the back of his neck, and he looked up to see Hunt coming his way.

The detective looked tired, his shirt rumpled and tie askew.

"Long day keeping the streets of San Francisco safe?" Vander asked.

Hunt grunted. "I know you help out with that. Usually by skirting the law."

"Who, me?" Vander said, deadpan.

Hunt snorted again and sipped his drink.

"Coffee?" Vander raised a brow.

"Got to head back to the station after. Vander, you know Trucker Patterson, right?"

Vander stiffened. Not Trucker, again. "Yeah. Asshole of epic proportions."

"But you have dealings with him and the Iron Wanderers."

Vander stayed silent, waiting to see where Hunt was heading with this line of conversation.

The detective turned to him. "We both know you keep your fingers on the pulse of all the players in the city."

"It pays to know what everyone's up to." It was how Vander kept control of his little slice of the world. He had a strong network of informants, and Ace could access just about anything, and that let Vander do his bit to protect his city.

"You're a powerbroker in San Francisco. You can

connect people, broker deals, and scare the shit out of people when required," Hunt said.

"Where are you going with this?"

Some party guests jostled them. A woman laughed and Vander saw they were...sucking on candy that was shaped like pacifiers.

"Let's talk on Ace's roof deck," Hunt suggested.

They hit the stairs. When Vander stepped onto the deck, a warm breeze tugged at his hair. Ace had a killer view of the city sprawl, and the water in the distance.

"The Wanderers are running drugs," Hunt said.

A muscle ticked in Vander's jaw. "I know, but Trucker keeps it to his club and close contacts. He knows if he sells that shit on the streets, or to kids, he'll have problems."

Hunt shook his head. "It's my job to make sure he doesn't sell that shit at all."

"And we both know that life isn't always black and white, Hunt. Your laws hinder you as much as they help."

"You keep playing God, Vander, you'll be tempted to step over the line."

"I have good balance," Vander said.

Hunt blew out a breath. "Trucker's also running weapons. Building up a little arsenal."

Vander stiffened. "Really?"

"He's keeping it very quiet. We arrested a low-level member who let it slip."

Fuck. Then Vander took another sip of beer. "He wants a war."

"He's got problems with the Burning Devils MC. But

I'm also getting whispers that he's got out-of-town interest. Looking to muscle in."

Vander's mouth flattened. They didn't need out-of-towners trying to strong-arm their way in.

"Word is, this new player wants to expand the drug trade."

Hell, no. "I'll handle it."

"Let the law try, first."

"You need proof that will hold up in court. I don't. Your way will take too long."

"Not if I have someone undercover in the club."

Vander cocked his head. "That's a dangerous game. If Trucker sniffs them out, he'll send them back in pieces."

"You owe me quite a few favors."

Fuck. Vander knew where this was going. "Hunt—"

"Lots. I've cleaned up after you and your guys numerous times."

"And I've helped you in return."

"I know, but you still cause me headaches."

Vander blew out a breath.

"Trucker trusts you," Hunt said.

"No, he doesn't."

"Okay, he's scared of you. I need you to vouch for my undercover officer and help them get into the Wanderers."

Shit. "They get found out, they're dead."

"They won't." Hunt paused. "Remember, you owe me."

Vander scraped a hand through his hair. "Fine. Your guy better be good."

"She is."

Vander stiffened. *A woman?* "No."

"Yes. Come to the station tomorrow, and we'll talk." Hunt headed for the stairs. "Bye, Vander."

Vander felt like throwing his beer bottle. He took another sip, instead. Some female cop wanted to prance into the most dangerous motorcycle club in the city, it wasn't his problem.

The beer tasted like oil.

Fuck. He headed back inside.

MAGGIE SAID goodbye to the last of their guests, standing at the front door of Ace's house.

No, *their* house.

She smiled and kicked off her shoes. She was still getting used to the fact that this was her home now, too.

But she'd never been happier. She lifted her hand and looked at her gorgeous ring. Really, really happy.

She headed up the stairs. The living room was mostly clean, thanks to her mom, Ace's mom, and Gia and the others who'd cleaned up most of the detritus from the party before they'd left. The dishwasher was humming quietly in the kitchen.

Maggie pressed a hand to her belly. She wasn't showing much, and she was desperate to have a big baby belly.

There was no sign of Ace.

"You'd better not be sleeping, Oliveira." She raised her voice. "There's still some cleanup to do."

He appeared in the hall, smiling, and she took a moment to appreciate her man.

Her fiancé.

The father of her baby.

The love of her life.

He'd ditched his shoes, too, and his shirt was untucked, his sleeves rolled up.

Heat ran through her, making her flush. She wanted to bite him. An unexpected side effect of the pregnancy hormones—she was horny all the time.

They were having so much sex it was a wonder they could both walk.

Ace's lips quirked and he studied her face. "*Gatinha*, I fucked you twice before I left for work this morning."

She rubbed her thighs together and squirmed. "So? That was hours ago."

He yanked her close and kissed her brains out. She clung to him, sucking on his tongue before sinking her teeth into his bottom lip.

As her hand moved to his belt, he grabbed her wrist.

"You're going have to wait a little bit, then I'll take care of you. I have a gift for you."

"A gift? We have a mountain of baby gifts in the living room waiting to be opened. Our kid won't need anything until he or she goes to college."

Ace grinned and twined his fingers with hers. "Come on." He towed her down the hall.

"Ace, I—"

He pulled her into one of the guest rooms and her heart stuttered.

"Oh..."

He'd set up the nursery.

"When did you do this?"

"This morning when you were at work. Obviously, I had help."

Maggie turned slowly. It was gorgeous. Just what they'd talked about. Cream walls, with a lovely, wooden crib that she'd admired online. The wall behind the crib had a pattern on it. Her heart squeezed. Tiny helicopters and computers.

A fluffy rug covered the floor, and a comfy, brown rocking chair sat in the corner. There were accents in a pale moss-green—a pillow on the chair, a blanket draped over the crib.

"The gang all helped me with decorating and putting things together. I'm not sure if you know this, but Gia is bossy."

"She says it's exceptional leadership skills." Maggie turned to the framed photos on the other wall. They were some of her photos—the city at sunrise, the Golden Gate Bridge, the Painted Ladies.

She met his gaze. "Ace, I love it. I can't believe you did this for me."

"For us. The three of us. And you can still add your touches, if you want. I knew it's been stressing you out, trying to find time to do everything."

"It's *perfect*." She wrapped her arms around him and pressed her cheek to his chest. "You're perfect."

He kissed the top of her head. "Even when we fight?"

They did argue sometimes. They both kind of got off on it. They'd argue, and then it would end with crazy monkey sex on the floor, the couch, the kitchen island, and one memorable time, on the desk in his office.

"Even then." She looked up. "When I look ahead, I can't imagine my life without you in it."

His eyes churned with emotion. "I feel the same way, Maggie. You make me laugh, you turn me on, you listen to me, you argue with me and you love me."

"Get used to it, Oliveira. I'm not planning to stop."

"Good. With you, I feel like I'm a better man." He touched his mouth to hers. The kiss turned hot and heavy, and his hands slid down her body. "Will you have my babies, *gatinha*?"

She laughed. "You didn't bother asking me the first time."

He cupped her ass and squeezed. "Still feeling horny?"

"All the time. Damn hormones."

"What do you need?" He had a sexy twinkle in his eye. "I'll give you whatever you want."

And he would. He'd protect her, and the children they made. He'd love her, care for her, and give her everything.

She wrapped her hand around his belt. "I just need you, Ace."

He swept her up into his arms and strode out, heading for their bedroom. "You've got me, Maggie. *Sempre*."

I hope you enjoyed Maggie and Ace's story!

Stay tuned for more Norcross Security. Vander's story, ***The Powerbroker***, is coming next month, November 2021.

Want to know more about Ace and Vander's time in New York? Then check out the first book in the **Billionaire Heists trilogy**, *Stealing from Mr. Rich* (Zane Roth's story). **Read on for a preview of the first chapter.**

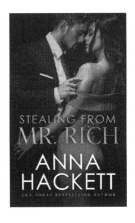

Don't miss out! For updates about new releases, free books, and other fun stuff, sign up for my VIP mailing list and get your *free box set* containing three action-packed romances.

Visit here to get started: www.annahackett.com

Would you like a FREE BOX SET of my books?

PREVIEW: STEALING FROM MR. RICH

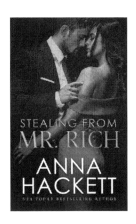

Monroe

The old-fashioned Rosengrens safe was a beauty.

I carefully turned the combination dial, then pressed closer to the safe. The metal was cool under my fingertips. The safe wasn't pretty, but stout and secure. There was something to be said for solid security.

Rosengrens had started making safes in Sweden over a hundred years ago. They were good at it. I listened to the pins, waiting for contact. Newer safes had internals made from lightweight materials to reduce sensory feedback, so I didn't get to use these skills very often.

Some people could play the piano, I could play a safe. The tiny vibration I was waiting for reached my fingertips, followed by the faintest click.

"I've gotcha, old girl." The Rosengrens had quite a few quirks, but my blood sang as I moved the dial again.

I heard a louder click and spun the handle.

The safe door swung open. Inside, I saw stacks of jewelry cases and wads of hundred-dollar bills. *Nice.*

Standing, I dusted my hands off on my jeans. "There you go, Mr. Goldstein."

"You are a doll, Monroe O'Connor. Thank you."

The older man, dressed neatly in pressed chinos and a blue shirt, grinned at me. He had coke-bottle glasses, wispy, white hair, and a wrinkled face.

I smiled at him. Mr. Goldstein was one of my favorite people. "I'll send you my bill."

His grin widened. "I don't know what I'd do without you."

I raised a brow. "You could stop forgetting your safe combination."

The wealthy old man called me every month or so to open his safe. Right now, we were standing in the home office of his expensive Park Avenue penthouse.

It was decorated in what I thought of as "rich, old man." There were heavy drapes, gold-framed artwork, lots of dark wood—including the built-in shelves around the safe—and a huge desk.

"Then I wouldn't get to see your pretty face," he said.

I smiled and patted his shoulder. "I'll see you next month, Mr. Goldstein." The poor man was lonely. His wife had died the year before, and his only son lived in Europe.

"Sure thing, Monroe. I'll have some of those donuts you like."

We headed for the front door and my chest tightened. I understood feeling lonely. "You could do with some new locks on your door. I mean, your building has top-notch security, but you can never be too careful. Pop by the shop if you want to talk locks."

He beamed at me and held the door open. "I might do that."

"Bye, Mr. Goldstein."

I headed down the plush hall to the elevator. Everything in the building screamed old money. I felt like an imposter just being in the building. Like I had "daughter of a criminal" stamped on my head.

Pulling out my cell phone, I pulled up my accounting app and entered Mr. Goldstein's callout. Next, I checked my messages.

Still nothing from Maguire.

Frowning, I bit my lip. That made it three days since I'd heard from my little brother. I shot him off a quick text.

"Text me back, Mag," I muttered.

The elevator opened and I stepped in, trying not to

worry about Maguire. He was an adult, but I'd practically raised him. Most days it felt like I had a twenty-four-year-old kid.

The elevator slowed and stopped at another floor. An older, well-dressed couple entered. They eyed me and my well-worn jeans like I'd crawled out from under a rock.

I smiled. "Good morning."

Yeah, yeah, I'm not wearing designer duds, and my bank account doesn't have a gazillion zeros. You're so much better than me.

Ignoring them, I scrolled through Instagram. When we finally reached the lobby, the couple shot me another dubious look before they left. I strode out across the marble-lined space and rolled my eyes.

During my teens, I'd cared about what people thought. Everyone had known that my father was Terry O'Connor—expert thief, safecracker, and con man. I'd felt every repulsed look and sly smirk at high school.

Then I'd grown up, cultivated some thicker skin, and learned not to care. *Fuck 'em.* People who looked down on others for things outside their control were assholes.

I wrinkled my nose. Okay, it was easier said than done.

When I walked outside, the street was busy. I smiled, breathing in the scent of New York—car exhaust, burnt meat, and rotting trash. Besides, most people cared more about themselves. They judged you, left you bleeding, then forgot you in the blink of an eye.

I unlocked my bicycle, and pulled on my helmet,

then set off down the street. I needed to get to the store. The ride wasn't long, but I spent every second worrying about Mag.

My brother had a knack for finding trouble. I sighed. After a childhood, where both our mothers had taken off, and Da was in and out of jail, Mag was entitled to being a bit messed up. The O'Connors were a long way from the Brady Bunch.

I pulled up in front of my shop in Hell's Kitchen and stopped for a second.

I grinned. *All mine.*

Okay, I didn't own the building, but I owned the store. The sign above the shop said *Lady Locksmith*. The logo was lipstick red—a woman's hand with gorgeous red nails, holding a set of keys.

After I locked up my bike, I strode inside. A chime sounded.

God, I loved the place. It was filled with glossy, warm-wood shelves lined with displays of state-of-the-art locks and safes. A key-cutting machine sat at the back.

A blonde head popped up from behind a long, shiny counter.

"You're back," Sabrina said.

My best friend looked like a doll—small, petite, with a head of golden curls.

We'd met doing our business degrees at college, and had become fast friends. Sabrina had always wanted to be tall and sexy, but had to settle for small and cute. She was my manager, and was getting married in a month.

"Yeah, Mr. Goldstein forgot his safe code again," I said.

Sabrina snorted. "That old coot doesn't forget, he just likes looking at your ass."

"He's harmless. He's nice, and lonely. How's the team doing?"

Sabrina leaned forward, pulling out her tablet. I often wondered if she slept with it. "Liz is out back unpacking stock." Sabrina's nose wrinkled. "McRoberts overcharged us on the Schlage locks again."

"That prick." He was always trying to screw me over. "I'll call him."

"Paola, Kat, and Isabella are all out on jobs."

Excellent. Business was doing well. Lady Locksmith specialized in providing female locksmiths to all the single ladies of New York. They also advised on how to keep them safe—securing locks, doors, and windows.

I had a dream of one day seeing multiple Lady Locksmiths around the city. Hell, around every city. A girl could dream. Growing up, once I understood the damage my father did to other people, all I'd wanted was to be respectable. To earn my own way and add to the world, not take from it.

"Did you get that new article I sent you to post on the blog?" I asked.

Sabrina nodded. "It'll go live shortly, and then I'll post on Insta, as well."

When I had the time, I wrote articles on how women —single *and* married—should secure their homes. My latest was aimed at domestic-violence survivors, and helping them feel safe. I donated my time to Nightingale House, a local shelter that helped women leaving DV situations, and I installed locks for them, free of charge.

"We should start a podcast," Sabrina said.

I wrinkled my nose. "I don't have time to sit around recording stuff." I did my fair share of callouts for jobs, plus at night I had to stay on top of the business-side of the store.

"Fine, fine." Sabrina leaned against the counter and eyed my jeans. "Damn, I hate you for being tall, long, and gorgeous. You're going to look *way* too beautiful as my maid of honor." She waved a hand between us. "You're all tall, sleek, and dark-haired, and I'm...the opposite."

I had some distant Black Irish ancestor to thank for my pale skin and ink-black hair. Growing up, I wanted to be short, blonde, and tanned. I snorted. "Beauty comes in all different forms, Sabrina." I gripped her shoulders. "You are so damn pretty, and your fiancé happens to think you are the most beautiful woman in the world. Andrew is gaga over you."

Sabrina sighed happily. "He does and he is." A pause. "So, do you have a date for my wedding yet?" My bestie's voice turned breezy and casual.

Uh-oh. I froze. All the wedding prep had sent my normally easygoing best friend a bit crazy. And I knew very well not to trust that tone.

I edged toward my office. "Not yet."

Sabrina's blue eyes sparked. "It's only *four* weeks away, Monroe. The maid of honor can't come alone."

"I'll be busy helping you out—"

"Find a date, Monroe."

"I don't want to just pick anyone for your wedding—"

Sabrina stomped her foot. "Find someone, or I'll find someone for you."

I held up my hands. "Okay, okay." I headed for my office. "I'll—" My cell phone rang. *Yes.* "I've got a call. Got to go." I dove through the office door.

"I won't forget," Sabrina yelled. "I'll revoke your best-friend status, if I have to."

I closed the door on my bridezilla bestie and looked at the phone.

Maguire. Finally.

I stabbed the call button. "Where have you been?"

"We have your brother," a robotic voice said.

My blood ran cold. My chest felt like it had filled with concrete.

"If you want to keep him alive, you'll do exactly as I say."

Zane

God, this party was boring.

Zane Roth sipped his wine and glanced around the ballroom at the Mandarin Oriental. The party held the Who's Who of New York society, all dressed up in their glittering best. The ceiling shimmered with a sea of crystal lights, tall flower arrangements dominated the tables, and the wall of windows had a great view of the Manhattan skyline.

Everything was picture perfect...and boring.

If it wasn't for the charity auction, he wouldn't be dressed in his tuxedo and dodging annoying people.

"I'm so sick of these parties," he muttered.

A snort came from beside him.

One of his best friends, Maverick Rivera, sipped his wine. "You were voted New York's sexiest billionaire bachelor. You should be loving this shindig."

Mav had been one of his best friends since college. Like Zane, Maverick hadn't come from wealth. They'd both earned it the old-fashioned way. Zane loved numbers and money, and had made Wall Street his hunting ground. Mav was a geek, despite not looking like a stereotypical one. He'd grown up in a strong, Mexican-American family, and with his brown skin, broad shoulders, and the fact that he worked out a lot, no one would pick him for a tech billionaire.

But under the big body, the man was a computer geek to the bone.

"All the society mamas are giving you lots of speculative looks." Mav gave him a small grin.

"Shut it, Rivera."

"They're all dreaming of marrying their daughters off to billionaire Zane Roth, the finance King of Wall Street."

Zane glared. "You done?"

"Oh, I could go on."

"I seem to recall another article about the billionaire bachelors. All three of us." Zane tipped his glass at his friend. "They'll be coming for you, next."

Mav's smile dissolved, and he shrugged a broad shoulder. "I'll toss Kensington at them. He's pretty."

Liam Kensington was the third member of their trio. Unlike Zane and Mav, Liam had come from money, although he worked hard to avoid his bloodsucking family.

Zane saw a woman in a slinky, blue dress shoot him a welcoming smile.

He looked away.

When he'd made his first billion, he'd welcomed the attention. Especially the female attention. He'd bedded more than his fair share of gorgeous women.

Of late, nothing and no one caught his interest. Women all left him feeling numb.

Work. He thrived on that.

A part of him figured he'd never find a woman who made him feel the same way as his work.

"Speak of the devil," Mav said.

Zane looked up to see Liam Kensington striding toward them. With the lean body of a swimmer, clad in a perfectly tailored tuxedo, he looked every inch the billionaire. His gold hair complemented a face the ladies oohed over.

People tried to get his attention, but the real estate mogul ignored everyone.

He reached Zane and Mav, grabbed Zane's wine, and emptied it in two gulps.

"I hate this party. When can we leave?" Having spent his formative years in London, he had a posh British accent. Another thing the ladies loved. "I have a contract to work on, my fundraiser ball to plan, and things to catch up on after our trip to San Francisco."

The three of them had just returned from a business trip to the West Coast.

"Can't leave until the auction's done," Zane said.

Liam sighed. His handsome face often had him voted the best-looking billionaire bachelor.

"Buy up big," Zane said. "Proceeds go to the Boys and Girls Clubs."

"One of your pet charities," Liam said.

"Yeah." Zane's father had left when he was seven. His mom had worked hard to support them. She was his hero. He liked to give back to charities that supported kids growing up in tough circumstances.

He'd set his mom up in a gorgeous house Upstate that she loved. And he was here for her tonight.

"Don't bid on the Phillips-Morley necklace, though," he added. "It's mine."

The necklace had a huge, rectangular sapphire pendant surrounded by diamonds. It was the real-life necklace said to have inspired the necklace in the movie, *Titanic*. It had been given to a young woman, Kate Florence Phillips, by her lover, Henry Samuel Morley. The two had run away together and booked passage on the Titanic.

Unfortunately for poor Kate, Henry had drowned when the ship had sunk. She'd returned to England with the necklace and a baby in her belly.

Zane's mother had always loved the story and pored over pictures of the necklace. She'd told him the story of the lovers, over and over.

"It was a gift from a man to a woman he loved. She was a shop girl, and he owned the store, but they fell in love, even though society frowned on their love." She sighed. "That's true love, Zane. Devotion, loyalty, through the good times and the bad."

Everything Carol Roth had never known.

Of course, it turned out old Henry was much older than his lover, and already married. But Zane didn't want to ruin the fairy tale for his mom.

Now, the Phillips-Morley necklace had turned up, and was being offered at auction. And Zane was going to get it for his mom. It was her birthday in a few months.

"Hey, is your fancy, new safe ready yet?" Zane asked Mav.

His friend nodded. "You're getting one of the first ones. I can have my team install it this week."

"Perfect." Mav's new Riv3000 was the latest in high-tech safes and said to be unbreakable. "I'll keep the necklace in it until my mom's birthday."

Someone called out Liam's name. With a sigh, their friend forced a smile. "Can't dodge this one. Simpson's an investor in my Brooklyn project. I'll be back."

"Need a refill?" Zane asked Mav.

"Sure."

Zane headed for the bar. He'd almost reached it when a manicured hand snagged his arm.

"Zane."

He looked down at the woman and barely swallowed his groan. "Allegra. You look lovely this evening."

She did. Allegra Montgomery's shimmery, silver dress hugged her slender figure, and her cloud of mahogany brown hair accented her beautiful face. As the only daughter of a wealthy New York family—her father was from *the* Montgomery family and her mother was a former Miss America—Allegra was well-bred and well-educated but also, as he'd discovered, spoiled and liked getting her way.

Her dark eyes bored into him. "I'm sorry things ended badly for us the other month. I was..." Her voice lowered, and she stroked his forearm. "I miss you. I was hoping we could catch up again."

Zane arched a brow. They'd dated for a few weeks, shared a few dinners, and some decent sex. But Allegra liked being the center of attention, complained that he worked too much, and had constantly hounded him to take her on vacation. Preferably on a private jet to Tahiti or the Maldives.

When she'd asked him if it would be too much for him to give her a credit card of her own, for monthly expenses, Zane had exited stage left.

"I don't think so, Allegra. We aren't...compatible."

Her full lips turned into a pout. "I thought we were *very* compatible."

He cleared his throat. "I heard you moved on. With Chip Huffington."

Allegra waved a hand. "Oh, that's nothing serious."

And Chip was only a millionaire. Allegra would see that as a step down. In fact, Zane felt like every time she looked at him, he could almost see little dollar signs in her eyes.

He dredged up a smile. "I wish you all the best, Allegra. Good evening." He sidestepped her and made a beeline for the bar.

"What can I get you?" the bartender asked.

Wine wasn't going to cut it. It would probably be frowned on to ask for an entire bottle of Scotch. "Two glasses of Scotch, please. On the rocks. Do you have Macallan?"

"No, sorry, sir. Will Glenfiddich do?"

"Sure."

"Ladies and gentlemen," a voice said over the loud-speaker. The lights lowered. "I hope you're ready to spend big for a wonderful cause."

Carrying the drinks, Zane hurried back to Mav and Liam. He handed Mav a glass.

"Let's do this," Mav grumbled. "And next time, I'll make a generous online donation so I don't have to come to the party."

"Drinks at my place after I get the necklace," Zane said. "I have a very good bottle of Macallan."

Mav stilled. "How good?"

"Macallan 25. Single malt."

"I'm there," Liam said.

Mav lifted his chin.

Ahead, Zane watched the evening's host lift a black cloth off a pedestal. He stared at the necklace, the sapphire glittering under the lights.

There it was.

The sapphire was a deep, rich blue. Just like all the photos his mother had shown him.

"Get that damn necklace, Roth, and let's get out of here," Mav said.

Zane nodded. He'd get the necklace for the one woman in his life who rarely asked for anything, then escape the rest of the bloodsuckers and hang with his friends.

Billionaire Heists

Stealing from Mr. Rich
Blackmailing Mr. Bossman
Hacking Mr. CEO

W ant to learn more about the mysterious, covert
Team 52? Check out the first book in the series,
Mission: Her Protection.

**When Rowan's Arctic research team pulls
a strange object out of the ice in Northern**

Canada, things start to go wrong...very, very wrong. Rescued by a covert, black ops team, she finds herself in the powerful arms of a man with scary gold eyes. A man who vows to do everything and anything to protect her...

Dr. Rowan Schafer has learned it's best to do things herself and not depend on anyone else. Her cold, academic parents taught her that lesson. She loves the challenge of running a research base, until the day her scientists discover the object in a retreating glacier. Under attack, Rowan finds herself fighting to survive... until the mysterious Team 52 arrives.

Former special forces Marine Lachlan Hunter's military career ended in blood and screams, until he was recruited to lead a special team. A team tasked with a top-secret mission—to secure and safeguard pieces of powerful ancient technology. Married to his job, he's done too much and seen too much to risk inflicting his demons on a woman. But when his team arrives in the Arctic, he uncovers both an unexplained artifact, and a young girl from his past, now all grown up. A woman who ignites emotions inside him like never before.

But as Team 52 heads back to their base in Nevada, other hostile forces are after the artifact. Rowan finds herself under attack, and as the bullets fly, Lachlan vows to protect her at all costs. But in the face of danger like they've never seen before, will it be enough to keep her alive.

Team 52
Mission: Her Protection
Mission: Her Rescue
Mission: Her Security
Mission: Her Defense
Mission: Her Safety
Mission: Her Freedom
Mission: Her Shield
Also Available as Audiobooks!

Want to learn more about *Treasure Hunter Security*? Check out the first book in the series, *Undiscovered*, Declan Ward's action-packed story.

One former Navy SEAL. One dedicated archeologist. One secret map to a fabulous lost oasis.

Finding undiscovered treasures is always daring, dangerous, and deadly. Perfect for the men of Treasure Hunter Security. Former Navy SEAL Declan Ward is haunted by the demons of his past and throws everything he has into his security business—Treasure Hunter Security. Dangerous archeological digs – no problem. Daring expeditions – sure thing. Museum security for invaluable exhibits – easy. But on a simple dig in the Egyptian desert, he collides with a stubborn, smart archeologist, Dr. Layne Rush, and together they get swept into a deadly treasure hunt for a mythical lost oasis. When an evil from his past reappears, Declan vows to do anything to protect Layne.

Dr. Layne Rush is dedicated to building a successful career—a promise to the parents she lost far too young. But when her dig is plagued by strange accidents, targeted by a lethal black market antiquities ring, and artifacts are stolen, she is forced to turn to Treasure Hunter Security, and to the tough, sexy, and too-used-to-giving-orders Declan. Soon her organized dig morphs into a wild treasure hunt across the desert dunes.

Danger is hunting them every step of the way, and Layne and Declan must find a way to work together...to not only find the treasure but to survive.

Treasure Hunter Security
Undiscovered
Uncharted
Unexplored
Unfathomed

Untraveled
Unmapped
Unidentified
Undetected
Also Available as Audiobooks!

Treasure Hunter Security

Undiscovered

Uncharted

Unexplored

Unfathomed

Untraveled

Unmapped

Unidentified

Undetected

Also Available as Audiobooks!

Eon Warriors

Edge of Eon

Touch of Eon

Heart of Eon

Kiss of Eon

Mark of Eon

Claim of Eon

Storm of Eon

Soul of Eon

King of Eon

Also Available as Audiobooks!

Galactic Gladiators: House of Rone

Sentinel

Defender

Centurion

Paladin

Guard

Weapons Master

Also Available as Audiobooks!

Galactic Gladiators

Gladiator

Warrior

Hero

Protector

Champion

Barbarian

Beast

Rogue

Guardian

Cyborg

Imperator

Hunter

Also Available as Audiobooks!

Hell Squad

Marcus

Cruz

Gabe

Reed

Roth

Noah

Shaw

Holmes

Niko

Finn

Devlin

Theron

Hemi

Ash

Levi

Manu

Griff

Dom

Survivors

Tane

Also Available as Audiobooks!

The Anomaly Series

Time Thief

Mind Raider

Soul Stealer

Salvation

Anomaly Series Box Set

The Phoenix Adventures

Among Galactic Ruins

At Star's End

In the Devil's Nebula

On a Rogue Planet

Beneath a Trojan Moon

Beyond Galaxy's Edge

On a Cyborg Planet

Return to Dark Earth

On a Barbarian World

Lost in Barbarian Space

Through Uncharted Space

Crashed on an Ice World

Perma Series

Winter Fusion

A Galactic Holiday

Warriors of the Wind

Tempest

Storm & Seduction

Fury & Darkness

Standalone Titles

Savage Dragon

Hunter's Surrender

One Night with the Wolf

For more information visit www.annahackett.com

ABOUT THE AUTHOR

I'm a USA Today bestselling romance author who's passionate about *fast-paced, emotion-filled* contemporary romantic suspense and science fiction romance. I love writing about people overcoming unbeatable odds and achieving seemingly impossible goals. I like to believe it's possible for all of us to do the same.

I live in Australia with my own personal hero and two very busy, always-on-the-move sons.

For release dates, behind-the-scenes info, free books, and other fun stuff, sign up for the latest news here:

Website: www.annahackett.com

Printed in Great Britain
by Amazon

86439689R00166